WHO IS MY NEIGHBOR?

SIGNS OF LIFE SERIES
BOOK 7

CRESTON MAPES

ALSO BY CRESTON MAPES

SIGNS OF LIFE SERIES

Signs of Life

Let My Daughter Go

I Pick You

Charm Artist

Son & Shield

Secrets in Shadows

Who is My Neighbor?

THE CRITTENDON FILES

Fear Has a Name

Poison Town

Sky Zone

ROCK STAR CHRONICLES

Dark Star: Confessions of a Rock Idol

Full Tilt

STAND ALONE THRILLERS

Celebrity Pastor

I Am In Here

Nobody

ACKNOWLEDGMENTS

Special thanks to author friend Robin Lee Hatcher for inviting me to join her Writing Sprints Group on Zoom, and all the friends I've made there. This group really helped me stay on track to finish book number fifteen.

Grateful for friend-author-cop Mark Mynheir for always being available to answer my questions about police procedures. Mark is a fine writer and devoted man of God. Thanks, brother.

High five to the Rosati's lunch group for brainstorming with me and coming up with some creative ideas.

To author friend Deb Raney, thank you for your time and insights about camper vans!

Thanks to Abigail Patel for her insights on pregnancy.

A shout out to my buddy Steve Warnstrom for his friendship and for giving me some important inside information for the book.

Thanks so much to my early reader team for your time and insights: Patty Mapes (wink, wink), Gail Mundy, Sharon Srock, Lynnelle Murrell, Rachel Savage, Vicki Burke, and Ginger Aster.

Narrator Drew Bott, thank you for bringing this story to life on audio once again and for making yourself available to narrate the entire series. I know you're a busy man.

WHO IS MY NEIGHBOR?

A Novel

1

———

IT WAS JUST minutes before the wedding ceremony on a damp, frigid December evening in Portland, Oregon. The father of the groom, Wayne Deetz, knew he had to get his head right. This was, after all, his son Brandon's big day; the first of their three adult kids to tie the knot. Deetz only wished for it to be under different circumstances.

The old stone church was crowded with the glowing faces of people whispering in anticipation, setting their big coats and parkas aside, and getting settled into the creaky pews for the nuptials. Dim lighting, the scent of fresh pine, flickering candles, and red carpet gave the church the undeniable feel of Christmas—just two weeks away.

The clean-shaven groom, Brandon Deetz, now twenty-five, stood stoically at the front of the church in a black tuxedo with his hands clasped in front of him, posture straight, staring down the long, candlelit aisle, awaiting the girl he'd asked to marry him just two months earlier, Kristen Trent.

The somber and somewhat distant look on Brandon's face made Deetz feel for his son. In a way, Brandon was sacrificing his life, his future for this young woman who had floated into their lives like a foreboding cloud.

Brandon was flanked by a melting pot of handsome groomsmen, including his towering best friend and police partner, Clarence

Waters, Mauricio, KJ, and Hwan. The slight priest, Father Hendricks, a close friend of the family, stood off to the side with his hands clasped at his chest. Deetz sat in the front pew next to wife Joanie and their two other adult children, Leena and J.P., along with J.P.'s long-time girlfriend, Tammy.

Deetz had noticed on his way down the aisle that Brandon's half of the church was packed, while Kristen's side was only about half full. That could probably be attributed to the fact that Kristen's past —and her mother's—were littered with baggage, bad decisions, and severed relationships. Deetz chastised himself for thinking that way, for being judgmental. Even though he knew those things to be true, he had to force himself to stop judging them and lamenting about the past. Kristen was about to become part of the family and she and Brandon would need their full support.

Deetz glanced at beautiful Joanie and wondered how she managed to shine through it all. Her faith was so strong, so real. She was trusting God to pave the way for Brandon and Kristen, to draw a line separating the past from the future. Yes, she'd had her moments of tears and doubts and anguish. She and Wayne had talked and cried together about Kristen's mental issues and surprise pregnancy. But, at some point during the last month, Joanie had silently resolved to embrace Kristen and the marriage that was about to proceed.

As the bridesmaids entered one by one, Deetz whispered to himself, urged himself to shake the disapproving thoughts that were haunting him with a heavy feeling of melancholy. Soon, Kristen would be coming down the aisle, escorted by her mother, Roxanne, and he needed to manufacture a pleasant smile at the very least.

Deetz remembered when Brandon told him he'd begun dating Kristen back in the spring. The father-son duo had been riding together with the Portland Police Bureau. Deetz, a seasoned investigator, had returned to uniform to ride with Brandon as part of the Bureau's mentorship program. That was over now. Brandon and Clarence were patrol officers and partners on the job, and Deetz was set to retire at the end of December after thirty-five years of service.

Brandon had told Deetz at the time that Kristen's father had left when she was a baby. They didn't know where he was, and they didn't want to know. Her mom then hit the booze hard and went through a number of toxic relationships with men, none of which had lasted. She was one of those down-and-out types, tough, no filter, gravelly smoker's voice.

The relationship between Brandon and Kristen had started off nicely, but after a few months, she began to get intensely jealous, without cause. Deetz would never forget the day Kristen showed up at the house when he was still recovering from a gunshot wound. They barely knew her, and she swept in like Mary Poppins, taking selfies with Deetz before he could even walk in the aftermath of the shooting. Brandon hadn't even known Kristen planned to visit, and he was freaked out by it; they all were.

It was then that Brandon told Kristen he wanted to cool it for a while. She went ballistic. She began to follow him. That's when J.P.'s girlfriend, Tammy, got involved and invited Kristen to the young adult group at her church; Kristen also began seeing a counselor several times a week.

"Hey." Joanie nudged Deetz. "Smile," she whispered. "You look like you're a million miles away. Come on. Be present."

"Sorry." He shifted in his seat, set his shoulders back, took a deep breath and exhaled. *Come on, come on, come on.*

Deetz leaned across Joanie and reached out his hand to daughter Leena, now twenty. "You look so beautiful," he whispered. Leena was on the autism spectrum and was living an amazing life. She was a supervisor at the Chick-fil-A restaurant where she'd worked since she was a teenager. She was able to drive and even dated a nice kid from work.

Leena squeezed Deetz's hand and pointed an accusing finger at him. "Mom says you better perk up."

Deetz rolled his eyes, shook his head, then leaned over further to J.P. and Tammy. "You both look amazing," he said. Tammy was stunning, and Deetz thought it probably wouldn't be long before those two were engaged.

Deetz turned back to the front of the church toward Brandon at the altar and kept looking at him until Brandon caught his eye. Deetz smiled proudly and nodded. Brandon blinked slowly and smiled back at his dad.

Kristen had informed Brandon two months earlier that she was pregnant, and Deetz knew Brandon was probably somewhat ashamed about it, although only the immediate family knew the secret.

The volume of the music arose distinctively; it was the sound of the Wedding March.

Everyone stood and turned to face the back of the church in anticipation of the bride.

Many of the Deetz's closest friends were there: Callie and Tyson Cooper; Joanie's best friend from Sedona, Suzanne Bartholomew; Sunny Carlisle; Portland Police Sergeant Dolby Tidwell, his wife Janet, and son Nick; and Deetz's longtime pals from the force who all sat together—Sid Sikorski, Angie Cook, Ben Briggs, and Virgil Bennett.

Joanie squeezed Deetz's hand. He glanced at her and they made eye contact—somehow knowing each other's every thought, fear, hope, and prayer—just as a tear trickled out the corner of Joanie's left eye.

All of the raw emotions—the good, the bad, the joyful, and the uncertainty of the future—swirled in Deetz's mind.

As the guests faced the rear of the church, Deetz remembered Brandon confiding in him that he had only "been with" Kristen once, in the heat of a moment that he wished had never happened.

One time is all it takes, buddy.

That nagged at Deetz on many levels. Brandon should have known better, should have been more careful, no, should have *wanted* to wait until they were married. Second, why did God allow this? The one time they were together and, boom, the trajectory of their lives was changed forever.

The troubling fact was, Brandon would not be marrying her now, this soon, if she had not been pregnant. That was what nagged at Deetz.

Kristen was still seeing a therapist but had quit attending Tammy's young adult group.

What had her father been like? Was he one of those bad seeds? He quite possibly could have had serious mental health issues that were hereditary and passed down to Kristen—and possibly to the baby.

Why are you doing this? All these 'what ifs' are just paranoia. Where's your faith?

As Kristen came into view, stepping slowly in rhythm with the March, her young face beamed. The crowd whispered their approval. Her wide smile was beautiful and genuine. She had distinct dimples, large brown eyes, long blond hair, and broad shoulders—a lovely young woman.

Her mother, Roxanne, was five inches shorter than Kristen and looked much older than her fifty-seven years of age. The booze and cigarettes had taken their toll. Their arms were locked as they marched. Her mom's dress was red, with lipstick to match, and she wobbled slightly on her high heels. Her eyes darted about the sanctuary, down toward her feet, at the Deetz family, and to Kristen, obviously feeling the weight of the many eyes upon her.

Of course, Kristen wasn't showing her pregnancy yet, but some people in the church probably guessed why the wedding had been arranged so quickly. Although he tried not to, Deetz *did* care what people must have thought. He was embarrassed by it. After all, he tried to live a Christian life and now his son was getting married because he'd gotten a girl pregnant. Like he heard the kids say all the time, it was "not a good look." But, then again, that was just Deetz's pride rearing its ugly head, and him feeling sorry for himself.

As Kristen and Roxanne made it to the front of the sanctuary, Father Hendricks, with his ruddy Irish cheeks, stepped forward, pushed his thick glasses up on his nose and smiled broadly. "Who gives this woman to be married to this man?"

The sanctuary fell silent.

Kristen shot Deetz and Joanie a confident grin and a tilt of the head. It was almost as if she was saying, "This *is* happening—whether you like it or not."

"I do," Roxanne said in a weak, cracking voice. She kissed Kristen on the cheek, leaving a hint of red lipstick, glanced at Deetz and Joanie, and plunked down in the pew with a loud sigh as if she was at a wrestling match.

"You may all be seated," said Father Hendricks.

Just as everyone settled into their seats and Brandon used his thumb to wipe the red lipstick from Kristen's cheek, voices erupted in the back foyer. Loud voices.

What now?

An adult male voice blurted something Deetz couldn't understand.

The volume and tone were sorely out of place. Something was definitely wrong.

Deetz's police instincts kicked in and he was turned around on the edge of his seat toward the noise as if he was about to rise. Joanie's hand touched his arm as if to say, "Let's wait and see."

Deetz now recognized the female voice of the wedding planner, Candace. "It's started. Everyone is seated!" she said, trying to keep her voice down.

Most every head was turned toward the back of the church now.

"You can and *will* let me in," the male voice boomed.

Deetz began to stand.

Suddenly, Candace was shoved backwards into the sanctuary, into everyone's view.

A large man darted past her, then slowed—like a child ducking past a restraint. He walked toward the front of the church. His pockmarked face was weatherworn, and he wore baggy, gray corduroy pants with badly wrinkled knees. He had on a brown plaid wool sport jacket with patches at the elbows, and his shoes were black faux leather with Velcro straps.

Candace stood at the back of the church with her mouth hanging open and her hands up in the air. Deetz was half-standing, half-sitting. He saw no weapon on the man and assumed he was going to duck into the first available seat.

The man's leathery face contorted from a quick, nervous smile to a proud look that said he was going to do whatever he wanted and he didn't care what anyone thought. He passed rows of open pews on Kristen's side of the church and continued walking toward the front to a growing number of murmurs from guests.

Deetz glanced over to see if he could tell whether Kristen or Roxanne recognized the man. Kristen appeared clueless and discombobulated.

Roxanne's hands covered her mouth, and her eyes grew to the size of saucers.

She knows him.

"You didn't think I'd miss my baby's wedding," the man said as he approached the bride and her mother.

Brandon took several steps toward the man.

Deetz stood and his cheeks warmed with embarrassment.

"Mom?" Kristen said, staring at the man in horror.

"My, my, my." The man stopped at the front of the church and held his arms out toward Kristen as if viewing a glowing pot of gold. "Kristen Ashley Trent. Aren't you a sight to behold."

"Roxanne?" Brandon held up his hands in question. "What's going on?"

Roxanne shook her head slightly, nervously, not making eye contact with the man, whom Deetz now assumed was Kristen's father.

"What do you mean, 'What's going on?'" the man said to Brandon. "You got a problem? You got a bone to pick with the father of the bride?"

He must be drunk.

The murmurs evolved into chatter, which spread through the pews like wildfire.

Deetz took several steps toward the man, but Father Hendricks held up his hands and raised his voice. "Everyone, be seated, please. Be seated, *now!*" He motioned dramatically with his arms for everyone to sit. "Bride and groom, step forward, please."

For a moment, time stood still.

Would the stranger do as Father Hendricks asked? Or was this thing about to erupt?

Kristen spun away from the man.

Brandon reached out his hand for hers. Father Hendricks quickly escorted them forward.

The man gave an evil glare toward Brandon, then Deetz and Joanie, tugged at the lapels of his old sports jacket, looked all around the church, and finally plunked down next to Roxanne, who buried her face in her hands.

Deetz slowly sat back down.

The man turned and stared at him with steely eyes.

"My name is Father Hendricks," the priest said loudly. "I have the distinct privilege of officiating this joyous ceremony today." His voice wavered slightly from the tension of the moment. "On behalf of Brandon and Kristen, welcome and thank you for being here."

The stranger leaned close to Roxanne and whispered something in her ear.

Roxanne set her shoulders back, shook her head, and looked away from him toward the front of the church.

"Brandon and Kristen are . . . thankful you are here to share in this wonderful moment in their lives."

All Deetz could think was, *what have we gotten ourselves into?*

2

———

AFTER THE AWKWARD scare at the wedding, Joanie was cautiously optimistic about how the reception was proceeding. People were talking, drinking, dancing, eating, and having a festive time. The outburst from the man at the church was in the rearview mirror—for now.

Since Kristen's mom had said she couldn't afford to pay for any of the affair—as the parents of the bride traditionally did—Joanie had taken it upon herself to find a location for the reception and sign the paperwork to pay the bill for the event. It was at a renovated leather manufacturing plant known as The Railroad, which was indeed next to an active railroad track just several blocks from the church. The building's original wood floors and brick walls had been exposed and restored, giving the event center a romantic, urban charm.

Kristen had practically insisted on a live band, so that's what they had (five pieces), along with plentiful hors d'oeuvres and a beautiful buffet featuring smoked salmon and roast beef, catered by the son of a friend of Joanie's. Ever since they'd arrived, Joanie and Wayne had not stopped talking to relatives and friends who'd come from near and far to celebrate the newlywed couple.

Joanie admired Wayne for the way he had graciously agreed to pay not only for the wedding reception, but also for the rehearsal dinner the previous night at their family favorite, Giovanni's Italian restaurant. As they had grown older together, Wayne had become more and more generous, which Joanie quietly delighted in. They had saved and invested for decades in order to pay for the kids' college educations, wedding events, and retirement, and now Wayne seemed to be letting the reigns out on their spending and giving.

The band was between songs and Joanie heard the sound of silverware tapping a glass and she turned to see who was proposing a toast—they'd already had several.

Ugh.

It was Randall Trent, the uninvited guest whom Roxanne had confirmed was indeed Kristen's biological father. It had become obvious in a short amount of time that Roxanne was completely shocked that Randall had shown up. Apparently, neither Roxanne nor Kristen had seen him since he'd abandoned them when Kristen was a baby. They all wondered how he even knew Kristen was getting married.

All Joanie wanted was for him to leave. He was a loose cannon and the one person in the room who had the potential to ruin the evening.

"Your attention please!" Randall said, standing and clinking the glass so hard Joanie thought it might shatter. "Your attention!" He took a long drink of red wine and wiped his mouth with the back of his pudgy hand.

When everyone saw who was speaking—the oddball who had interrupted the start of the wedding ceremony—the room fell silent, probably more out of curiosity than respect.

Joanie had to tell herself to relax and breathe.

Roxanne was seated next to Randall with a look of terror etched on her face as she stared at the white tablecloth and candles, and picked at the edge of a napkin that featured the words 'Kristen & Brandon' scripted in gold foil.

Randall raised a hand toward Kristen. "Is she not the most beautiful bride you've ever seen?"

Kristen cringed and squirmed to a smattering of applause, but not the kind of applause Randall had hoped for.

"I *sa-id,* isn't she the most beautiful bride you have ever seen?"

More applause now, just to appease the guy.

"That's better!" He cackled.

Joanie looked at Deetz, who was scowling.

Brandon glanced at Joanie, shook his head, then stared at the man with a threatening glare.

Please, Jesus, calm everyone down.

"Not many of you know me. My name is Randall Trent, proud father of the bride!"

He expected huge applause, but seeing the disgraced looks on Kristen's and Brandon's faces, the guests only whispered. No one clapped. And why should they? Anyone who knew the situation in the slightest knew this man had been absent for the past twenty-five years.

"Oh, so that's how it's going to be? That's how you welcome the long-lost father?" Randall said, slurring his words.

Joanie was on the edge of alarm.

Kristen stood abruptly, all eyes shifting to her. She hurried from the room as fast as she could, being careful not to trip over her long dress and heels. Several of the bridesmaids ran after her to the sounds of whispers and murmurs.

"Now look what you've done!" Randall said rudely, throwing a pointing finger toward where Kristen had exited. "We were about to have the father-daughter dance. You've ruined it. You people . . . I'm starting to wonder what kind of a family we've married into."

Several boos arose throughout the gathering, making Joanie cringe.

Wayne stood abruptly and headed toward Randall.

Oh, no, Joanie thought.

Brandon saw his dad moving toward Randall and stood up to follow as well.

"Brandon!" Joanie shook her head sternly at him and pointed for him to sit back down.

Brandon held his hands up innocently.

Joanie wasn't having it. She headed him off and got in his way.

"Let your father handle this," she said sternly.

"Mom, it's cool. Just let me go with Dad."

"The last thing we need is for you to get into a brawl with Kristen's father."

Brandon's best friend Clarence came up from behind and clapped his large hands onto Brandon's shoulders. "Listen to your mom, bro. Let your dad talk to the dude. He's obviously had too much to drink. Everybody just needs to chill."

The three of them stood there and turned toward Randall.

Deetz got to him and said, "Are you finished?"

Randall looked around the room and smirked. "You people."

"Why don't you take a seat," Deetz said. "Or, better yet, leave."

"A bunch of filthy rich . . ."

"We're not rich," Deetz snapped. "We've saved all our lives for this moment. And we're not about to let *you* ruin it. You're done giving toasts. And if I hear another word from you, I'll throw you out of here myself."

Randall's eyes went dead.

His wide mouth curled into a nasty frown.

His nostrils flared.

It was the face of someone who looked as if he had suddenly smelled a dead animal.

He slowly leaned over and picked up his wine glass. "So, this is how it's going to be? This is how you treat family?"

Deetz leaned closer to him. "You are not my family. As far as I can tell, Kristen doesn't even know you. I'm trying to figure out why you're even here."

Randall closed his eyes, smiled slightly, and grunted. "Let me say something to you, Deetz, that you need to hear very clearly. You and your boy, and your friendly little wife, and all your other fam-damily, *do not* want to get on my bad side. I urge you, don't do it. Because I got nothing else to do with my time than to plan and scheme how to make your lives *miserable.*"

Deetz inhaled deeply and let out a long sigh. Joanie new that look—he was weighing carefully what he was about to say. "We don't want any trouble with you, Trent. So, why don't you—"

"Well, I'm afraid you may have already found it." Randall turned toward the bar. "I'm going to excuse myself and get another drink of your booze, maybe get some more of that beef you've saved up all your life for. And then I'll make that toast I was going to make— before I was so rudely interrupted."

Randall huffed off toward the bar.

Joanie made her way over to Deetz.

"Well?" she said.

Deetz shook his head. "He's all worked up. Drunk," Deetz whispered and clasped Joanie's hand. "We just need to keep our cool and get through tonight."

3

———————

Deetz kept his eye on Randall Trent, who proceeded to do exactly what he said he was going to do. He hit the bar, downed a burgundy like it was water and ordered another, then headed directly to the end of the buffet where a server in a white uniform was slicing roast beef. Randall repeatedly jabbed his plate back at the server each time the man laid a slice on his plate, until they were five high. Then he smothered the rare beef in horseradish sauce, dripping a glob on the floor, and headed back to his seat, licking every finger.

Deetz noticed his oldest son, J.P., heading toward him.

"Hey, Pops." J.P. patted his dad on the shoulder.

"Hey, son."

J.P. examined his dad and followed his eyes toward where Randall was sitting, wolfing down his food.

"Word on the street is he's been shacking up with Kristen's mom," J.P. said.

Deetz's head spun. "What? Roxanne? Where'd you hear that?"

"Tammy heard it just now from one of her social worker friends who spends time with a couple clients in Roxanne's apartment building," J.P. said.

"I thought no one had seen the guy since Kristen was a baby," Deetz said.

J.P. shrugged his shoulders. "Apparently that was bad intel."

14

Deetz's eyes closed, he sighed and shook his head in disbelief. Roxanne couldn't be trusted.

"You're pretty wound up, Dad," J.P. said. "Relax. Enjoy this. That guy's harmless."

"I know. You're right. I just don't want him to ruin it for Brandon and Kristen—or your mom."

"Good evening, gentlemen." The low voice came from behind. It was Portland Police Sergeant Dolby Tidwell, Deetz's boss and long-time friend. "You throw a good party, Wayne."

They exchanged greetings, with J.P. and Tidwell getting caught up for a minute. Deetz noticed Tidwell wasn't drinking anything. He'd been on the wagon for months and looked better than he had in years. Tidwell was tall, bald, and built like a stone wall. His eyes were clear and his whole demeanor was energetic and upbeat. *Good for him.*

"So, what was that all about with the dude at the wedding?" Tidwell nodded toward Randall.

"He's Kristen's dad," J.P. said. "He left when she was a baby."

"This is supposedly the first time she's met him," Deetz said.

"No way," said Tidwell.

Deetz and J.P. both nodded.

"I hate to say it, but he looks familiar," Tidwell said. "Something about him . . ."

"Oh, great," Deetz said, knowing Tidwell never forgot a face.

"What's his name?" Tidwell said. "I'll run him through the database," meaning the Law Enforcement Data System (LEDS), Oregon's police database.

"Randall Trent," Deetz said, disgustedly.

"I'm surprised you didn't run him already," Tidwell said. "Brandon married this girl. I'd know everything about her."

"The guy was non-existent until tonight," Deetz said.

"Look at Leena," Tidwell said, pointing at Deetz's daughter, who was tearing up the dance floor. "She's having the time of her life. Good for her. I need to get out there and dance with her."

Tidwell and Leena had always had a special friendship. He looked out for her, and she treated him like an uncle.

"Tammy's right there with her," Deetz said.

"Isn't she a beauty?" J.P. said of his girlfriend.

"It won't be long till we're celebrating you guys," Tidwell said.

J.P. raised his eyebrows. "You never know."

"So, Wayne, only three more weeks. How does it feel?" Tidwell said.

Deetz shook his head and smiled. "I can't believe it's almost here. It feels good, Sarge. I'm ready."

"We're going to miss you," Tidwell said. "Think of all we've been through." Tidwell rested a big hand on Deetz's shoulder. "Have you put any more thought into my offer?"

"What's this?" J.P. said with surprise.

Tidwell tilted his head at J.P. as if he was surprised Deetz hadn't told him. "I asked your old man if he'd be the chaplain for the Bureau."

"What?" J.P. looked at his dad. "That's amazing. Are you gonna do it, Dad? What's it entail?"

Tidwell spoke up. "Basically, he'd be on call in real-time crisis situations, to visit officers who get hospitalized, help with death notifications, officer wellbeing, that kind of stuff. He'd be a perfect fit. And I told him he can work when he can work. It's a no-brainer if you ask me. He's made for it. What else are you gonna do all day, Wayne, sleep till noon and watch cooking shows?"

They all laughed.

"Are you going to do it, Dad?"

"I'm not sure," Deetz said. "I'm thinking about it."

"What's Mom say about it?" J.P. said.

Deetz shook his head and smiled. "She wants me to be done."

"Yeah," Tidwell said with a laugh. "See how she feels after you've been following her around the house for a couple weeks. She'll be begging you to do it!"

They all laughed and watched the activity on the dance floor.

"You ready for Monday?" Tidwell said.

Monday was when Deetz's replacement would show up for his first day with the Portland Police Bureau. His name was Howard Googan, a well-decorated police investigator from Seattle, whom Deetz would be training leading up to his retirement at the end of December.

"You mean, Googan? Sure," Deetz said.

"Did I tell you he just went through a divorce? That's why he's moving over here, to get away from the ex."

"I was in the interview, remember?" Deetz said.

"Oh, yeah, shoot, that's right," Tidwell said. "He was a little rough around the edges."

"*Now* you're saying that?" Deetz said. "I told you I wasn't comfortable with him."

"He's the best we could find. He has the experience," Tidwell said. "You saw what we had to choose from. Plus, he seems like good police."

Deetz shrugged. "It is what it is. I'll get him in shape."

Tidwell clapped the top of Deetz's shoulder. "That's what I want to hear. Just have him do everything you do and we'll hit it off fine."

Deetz looked toward Randall's table. The man was gone; his white cloth napkin crumpled on his empty plate. Deetz scanned the large room and spotted him at one of the bars again, this time, joking loudly with the bartenders—who didn't look amused—and then staggering away with two glasses of red wine. He found an empty high-top table next to the dance floor, set one glass down on the black tablecloth, and drank from the other. Two young ladies laughed their way to the dance floor, right in front of Randall's table, and he eyed them up and down, and yelled something at them.

Brandon must have heard what Randall said, because he left Kristen on the dance floor and approached Randall.

No!

"Excuse me, guys, I need to diffuse this," Deetz said to Tidwell and J.P.

On his way to the table, Deetz could tell Brandon was chewing out Randall, who responded by stepping closer to Brandon and shoving a finger in his face.

"What's going on?" Deetz said, heart pounding as he got there and stepped between the two men.

"He's drunk and harassing people," Brandon said, not looking at Deetz, but at Randall.

"Your boy here needs to back off before he gets his face smashed," Randall yelled over the music, spewing spittle as he did so.

Deetz turned Brandon aside, squared up with him and said, "Let me handle this, okay? Just go enjoy yourself. Don't worry about this. Please. It's okay."

"Daddy to the rescue," Randall said, wagging his fat head. "Why don't you let him take care of himself, Daddy Daycare?"

Brandon's nostrils flared, his lips pursed into a mean frown, and he glared at Deetz.

"Just go," Deetz said.

Brandon stormed off.

Deetz had had it.

"Come with me," Deetz said, grabbing Randall's left bicep.

Randall yanked his arm away from Deetz. "Get your hands off me." He swayed as he said it.

Deetz felt the heat rush to his face. He leaned close to Randall's ear and spoke over the music. "If you don't come outside peacefully with me, I'm going to arrest you right now for drunk and disorderly conduct, disturbing the peace, and whatever else I can think of."

Deetz stepped back and examined the man.

Randall scowled and shook his head, then downed the remainder of wine in his glass. He reached for the full glass on the table.

Deetz grabbed his wrist. "You won't need that. Let's go."

Randall was a large, oafish man. He reeked of alcohol and possibly a hint of body odor.

Someone grabbed Deetz's arm. He turned. It was Roxanne.

"What's going on?" she yelled over the music.

Randall smirked.

Deetz leaned over and spoke close to her ear. "We're going outside."

Roxanne shook her head. "No. Please. Let him stay, Wayne. He's fine. If he's anything like the old days, he gets a little rowdy when he drinks. But really, he's harmless. I'll keep an eye on him. I promise."

Deetz could tell she'd had too much to drink as well. He couldn't believe it. "He's drunk, Roxanne. He's making rude comments to the guests. I'm not going to let him ruin this evening."

She reached out and clasped Randall's arm. "We're going to

dance. I'll make sure he behaves." She pulled Randall toward the dance floor. "I promise. He's fine. Please, forgive us."

It was such an awkward moment. Roxanne was the mother of the bride. Deetz didn't want to get into an argument with her in the middle of the wedding reception, and he didn't want to drive a wedge in the relationship.

Reluctantly, he let them go.

Randall shot one last glance at Deetz, then threw his big head back and laughed.

4

JOANIE WONDERED what was going on as she watched Roxanne lead Randall away from Deetz, onto the dance floor, both walking unsteadily. Just then, the band launched into a popular Bruno Mars song. Many guests in the large room who hadn't been dancing now headed for the dance floor like ants converging on a picnic.

Brandon and Kristen danced together right up in front of the band, surrounded by friends, and Joanie hoped Roxanne and Randall would keep their distance.

"Come on, Mom," Leena called and held out a hand toward Joanie, as she and J.P. and Tammy headed out to the dance floor. "You've got to dance to this!"

Joanie looked around for Deetz, but he'd vanished.

She loved to dance and followed Leena onto the crowded floor. They weaved their way through the crowd to the beat of the music, right up to Brandon and Kristen, who greeted them warmly. The music was too loud to hear each other. Clarence's and Brandon's other buddies made a big deal over Leena and Joanie, who laughed and danced.

The music pulsed loudly and Joanie felt the bass beating in her chest. People were loose and laughing and dancing their hearts out. It was turning out to be a wonderful celebration among family and friends. Kristen was an especially good dancer. She and Brandon held hands off and on, clapped, kissed, and moved with the upbeat rhythm of the music.

When Randall busted through the crowd, followed by Roxanne, Joanie gasped and tried not to show her apprehension. Instead, she danced to her left about five feet, trying to turn the newlywed couple away from Randall and Roxanne.

It worked momentarily.

And then Randall danced his way over until he was right beside Brandon and Kristen.

Joanie's heart raced and she scanned the room for Wayne. There he was, standing with Tidwell off to the side, but clearly alert to what was going on.

Brandon and Kristen noticed Randall, looked at each other, and their countenance deflated at the same instant.

Randall continued to dance, leaned toward them, and yelled something Joanie could not understand.

Kristen immediately leaned back and shook her head and said, "No."

Randall laughed and reached out and took her hand.

She pulled it away with a look of shock and disgust.

Brandon stepped in and yelled for Randall to back off.

They weren't dancing anymore.

Joanie had stopped, too, but the band played on.

She was infuriated by this man, this stranger who'd shown up out of nowhere only hours ago and was wreaking havoc on one of the most important days of their lives.

Roxanne was tugging at Randall's arm, trying to get him to leave the floor with her. But she had all the effect of a fly on a buffalo.

Brandon looked as if he was about to unload on the man.

Joanie approached Randall, the music still loud.

She pushed him toward Roxanne. "Go with her!" Joanie said. "Just go! We don't want any trouble."

Randall laughed in her face.

When Brandon saw his tiny mom trying to push the giant intruder, he was between them in a flash. He urged Joanie to go back to her table.

Then the song ended.

A large group of guests stood, watching with mouths and eyes open wide.

Deetz and Tidwell made their way to the edge of the dance floor and looked as if they were about to escort Randall from the building.

Randall approached the lead singer of the band, exchanged some dialogue, and took the microphone. He tapped it several times and the sound was heard echoing over the speakers.

"Ladies and gentlemen, your attention, please." Randall's deep voice boomed over the sound system. When the guests realized who had the mic, the room fell silent and everyone stopped to watch. "The wait is over. The father of the bride and the lovely bride will now dance the traditional father-daughter dance." He handed the mic back to the musician, turned around, and dramatically extended an arm toward Kristen.

As the band launched into *Isn't She Lovely* by Stevie Wonder, Kristen clasped her hands in front of her mouth and looked at Brandon sheepishly. Brandon leaned over and said something to her. She leaned back and looked at him again. Brandon said something more to her.

Meanwhile, Randall made his way to Kristen. "Shall we?"

Kristen looked around at all the guests, who slowly backed up to make a space on the dance floor and waited with bated breath to see what Kristen would do.

What an awful situation.

It felt as if everyone was silently hoping for peace between Kristen and her father.

Roxanne stepped forward, nodding at Kristen with outstretched arms toward her and Randall, suggesting they come together for the dance.

Kristen appeared frozen. Roxanne touched her elbow.

Reluctantly, Kristen stepped toward Randall.

He took her right hand in his left, drew her toward him, and they began to slow dance.

With a sigh of relief, Joanie went over and stood with Brandon and his friends.

"I told her it was up to her," Brandon said in his mom's ear. "If she'd said no, it could have really exploded."

"You did the right thing," Joanie said.

Randall beamed as he led Kristen slowly around the dance floor.

Kristen, on the other hand, looked around the room stoically at all the guests and barely made eye contact with the man who called himself her father.

Joanie slipped away from the dance floor to check the buffet and was pleased to see that the catering team had done an excellent job of keeping plenty of hot food out. Everything looked fresh and delicious. She hadn't eaten much so she grabbed a stuffed mushroom and several pieces of cheese and turned around to see Tyson and Callie Cooper approaching with their winter coats over their arms.

"We just wanted to tell you what a lovely evening it was," Callie said.

"Everything was perfect," Tyson added. "Thank you for letting us celebrate with you."

Joanie wondered what they'd thought of the strange intruder, she wondered what *everyone* had thought, but it was out of her hands. She was determined to let it go. "Thank you for being here, you two," she said. "We're so glad you could come. Drive safely."

They were off.

As they bundled up and headed out the vestibule into the winter night, Joanie could feel a wisp of cold air blow in. She smelled cigarette smoke. Outside, she noticed Deetz's long-time police colleague, Angie Cook, smoking a cigarette. She wore a full-length black winter coat, a dark hat, and had her arms wrapped around her chest. Every breath sent a puff of steam into the night air.

When Joanie turned around to look for Wayne, she knew instantly something was wrong.

Wayne and Sergeant Tidwell were throwing on their winter coats and walking briskly toward Joanie. The other law enforcement guests—Sid, Ben, and Virgil—walked quickly beside them as Tidwell explained something to them.

They got to Joanie and she squared up with Wayne and asked what was wrong.

Deetz's shoulders dropped and, with a look of sorrow, he said, "Our house got broken into—"

"What?"

"I'm sorry, honey, I've got to go. But don't worry. Everything will be fine. I'll take care of it."

"How bad?" Joanie said, hearing the panic in her own voice. "How do you know?"

"Dispatch called me. The Enochs saw a van in our driveway and called 911," Deetz said, referring to their neighbors. "By the time our guys got there the van was gone. They broke into the front door. I don't know any more yet."

Deetz turned around and searched the dance floor, probably for Brandon and Kristen, then looked back at Joanie. "Don't let it ruin the night for them. When they notice I'm gone just explain what happened. No one's hurt. Whoever did it is gone. It'll be okay. I'll call with an update as soon as I can."

Joanie's heart broke.

What had they taken? How bad was the damage?

Wayne would miss the big send-off.

She looked out over the dance floor and her gaze settled on the large, uncouth stranger, Randall Trent. Somehow, she couldn't help but think that he was a big, bad curse and that he was to blame for Wayne having to leave.

Just then, Roxanne walked up and embraced Randall. They staggered and laughed.

What a pair, she thought.

Welcome to the family.

5

———

IT WAS DARK AND A COLD, steady rain was falling. Deetz and Tidwell were met out front of Deetz's house by the two officers who'd initially received the radio call about the "strange van in the driveway," as reported by the Enochs, next door. The officers' names were Metzger and Small, and Deetz knew them, but not well.

"Looks like they used a crowbar or something similar to get in the front door," Small said. "The good news is, we couldn't find much that's been disturbed."

"Where's forensics?" Tidwell said. "They should be here by now."

"They'll be here soon, Sarge," said Metzger. "They're spread thin tonight, and there was a homicide just before this, in town."

"Yeah, I heard," Tidwell said. "Have you checked all the other doors and around the outside of the house?"

"Affirmative, Sarge. We can't find anything out of order," said Small. "We were hoping to find some footprints in the wet grass, but nothing so far. It looks like there aren't any security cameras."

Tidwell's head turned toward Deetz with a look as if to say, "Are you kidding me, Wayne?"

Deetz shook his head and stepped inside the house feeling like an idiot. Joanie had suggested a security camera several times over the past year or so, especially after the last death threat Deetz got

25

during a trial involving notorious gangster and drug lord Sidney Grimaldi. And Tidwell had told him recently he was surprised Deetz had never installed any sort of security camera, even the simple doorbell kind. Deetz chastised himself—thinking those had probably been hints from God that he'd ignored.

He proceeded through the downstairs turning on lights as he went, surprised he wasn't seeing any damage, or anything amiss. He kept thinking that whoever had done this may have known that no one was going to be home that night, because of the wedding.

"I'll go upstairs, Wayne," said Tidwell, whose heavy footsteps seemed to shake the house as he pounded up the stairs.

Deetz stopped and stared at a plastic jug of milk that sat on the kitchen island. A drinking glass sat beside it with about an inch of milk in it. Next to that was the colorful paper chain Joanie had made for Deetz more than a year ago. It had started out with over four hundred rings on it, each ring representing another day closer to his retirement. He'd torn off one ring each day since she'd given it to him, and now there were less than twenty remaining.

Deetz leaned in for a closer look but didn't see any lip marks around the rim of the glass, or fingerprints. He would have forensics dust both, as well as the handles of the refrigerator. Surely, they would find some DNA.

Next, he grabbed a tissue and made his way into the master bedroom and crossed to Joanie's jewelry box. He used the tissue to open the lid and the drawers, and it appeared as full as ever, but she would need to check for specifics.

As he hurried into the walk-in closet, he was getting an eerie feeling about the break-in. *Why didn't they take anything?* It was as if they had come in and quietly looked around. Deetz had made a mental list of his most personal enemies over his thirty-five years of fighting crime in Portland. *Any one of those psychos could be behind this.*

He got down on his hands and knees, pushed aside the laundry basket, and examined the small, shiny black safe that he had bolted to the wall years ago. Using the tissue, he quickly punched in the code, opened it, and peered in. Everything was there: two handguns and their respective magazines, an envelope of cash and bonds, and several small boxes of gold coins.

"Why did you come here?" he whispered as he shut the safe,

pushed the laundry basket back in place, got to his feet, and went back out to the living room.

"The forensics team is seven minutes out, Investigator Deetz," said Metzger.

"Good. Thanks," Deetz said. "I'll be upstairs."

Because their main living quarters—kitchen and master bedroom—were on the first floor, and J.P. and Brandon had moved out, Leena's bedroom and bathroom were the only rooms that got any use upstairs.

Tidwell had the second floor lit up like a stadium.

"Sure is clean up here," Tidwell said, as Deetz met him in the hallway.

"Leena's the only one who comes up here," Deetz said. "Did you find anything?"

"No. I wonder if they even came up here. Maybe something scared them off."

Deetz told Tidwell about the milk and glass as he went into Leena's room, only to find everything looking the way it always did. He ducked into the bathroom and found the same. Next, he went into what were formerly the boys' bedrooms but were now guest rooms. Nothing seemed amiss.

"Anything missing downstairs?" Tidwell said.

"Not that I can tell. Pretty weird."

"Yeah."

They made their way back downstairs.

"Wayne, I can take it from here with forensics if you want to go back to the reception," Tidwell said.

Deetz checked his watch and thought about it. He wanted to make sure the entire place was dusted thoroughly for prints and DNA. He knew Tidwell would see to that, but by the time he'd get back to the reception it would be over.

"Investigator Deetz," Small called. "Your neighbor's at the door. The one who called us—a Mr. Enoch."

Deetz crossed to the foyer. "Come in, Brodie. Nasty night out there."

Brodie and Jeanette Enoch had moved into the house next door several months ago. The man stepped inside, wiped his waterproof Merrell's on the carpeted rug, pulled back the wet hood of his navy parka, and looked all around. "So, someone did break in after all?"

"Yep." Deetz pointed to the splintered doorframe. "But we can't find anything missing. What exactly did you see?"

"A dark van. It was unmarked and backed in, so I thought I better call 911." Brodie was a lanky guy, mid- to late-forties, the outdoorsy hiker type. He had short dark curly hair and a severe face, with a chiseled jaw and veins protruding at his temple and neck.

"Thanks for being so observant," Deetz said. "How far was it backed in?"

"Right up to the garage." Brodie blinked involuntarily, as he often did. It was some kind of tic.

"Did you see who was driving or how many there were?"

Brodie shook his head. "The windows were dark."

"Did it have a lot of windows or was it one of those with no windows?"

"No, just driver and front passenger windows," Brodie said. "I saw it when I came home from getting a pizza. I knew you guys had the wedding, so I thought I better call the police. We don't have a good vantage point from our house, so I couldn't see once I was in our house. Maybe the Dorcetts or Morgans saw something."

"Yeah, we'll see," Deetz said, knowing they hadn't because both couples were at Brandon's wedding. The Enochs hadn't been invited because Wayne and Joanie barely knew them.

"Did you happen to notice the license plate?" Tidwell said.

Brodie twitched. "No, no I didn't . . . but it was backed in, so—"

"Right. You couldn't have seen it anyway. Do you happen to know how long they were here?"

Brodie frowned and shook his head. "I didn't even know it was anything for sure. To be honest, once I called it in, I just let them handle it. Sorry about that. I really didn't think it was anything. In this neighborhood? We heard it was so safe."

"It always has been."

Deetz felt rather awkward the few times he'd been around Brodie, who he thought was on the strange side. Brodie would seek out Joanie when she was working in the yard or getting the mail in order to strike up conversations, but he seemed to avoid Deetz.

Wayne sometimes joked that Brodie was stalking Joanie—a woman some fifteen years his senior.

"I hope you didn't have to miss any of the wedding or festivities," Brodie said.

Deetz shrugged. "Yeah, unfortunately, the reception was still going on when we got the call."

"Oh, I'm sorry to hear that. But Joanie stayed?"

There he goes again.

"Yeah," Deetz said, pulling his phone out of his pocket. "In fact, I need to call her to fill her in. Listen, thanks for coming over, neighbor. And thanks for calling it in. We appreciate you looking out for us."

"Always, always," Brodie said, slipping on his hood and turning for the door. "I'm sorry this happened. Oh, by the way, we have a gift for the bride and groom. We'll get it over soon."

As Brodie dashed off into the freezing night, headlights turned into the driveway.

Forensics had arrived.

6

BRANDON AND KRISTEN were supposed to be headed to The Ritz-Carlton in downtown Portland for the night, before catching their flight the next morning to Hawaii for their honeymoon. On the way to the Ritz, it was Kristen who read Brandon's mind and suggested they stop by the house to check in on Deetz in the aftermath of the break-in.

When Brandon pulled his Jeep into the driveway—complete with "Just Married!" painted all over it, and cans on strings clanging from the back—he saw his dad peer through a front window and cross to the door.

"What are you doing here?" Deetz called from the front door, as Brandon helped Kristen out of the Jeep with her long white dress in tow.

The couple clung to each other as they hurried through the cold and drizzle and stepped inside the warm foyer.

"What a night," Brandon said, noticing the splintered doorframe.

Deetz gave them each a hug and apologized for leaving the reception early and missing their send-off. "How was it?" he asked.

They looked at each other, paused, and laughed.

"It was a night to remember, let's put it that way," Brandon said.

"My *dad* made another big scene as we were getting ready to leave," Kristen said. "What an embarrassment. I'm so sorry he showed up, Wayne. Truly. I didn't know he was in town. Apparently, my mom did. She's got some explaining to do."

"We'll tell you about the send-off later," Brandon said, looking around the house. "So, what went down here?"

"Come into the kitchen," Deetz said, leading the way. "Can I get you guys anything?"

"Just water, Dad," Brandon said.

With his dress shirt untucked and his tie loosened, Deetz served waters and explained what had happened as the newlyweds sat on barstools at the island.

"Forensics couldn't find anything. Nothing. Whoever it was had on gloves of some kind."

"There was no DNA on the glass?" Brandon said.

Deetz shook his head. "It's so weird. They poured a glass of milk and didn't drink any of it."

"And you haven't found anything missing?" Kristen said.

"Nothing. We're wondering if something scared them off."

"Well, I guess now you'll finally get a security camera," Brandon said, sarcastically.

"Don't remind me. Your mom and Tidwell have both nagged me about that . . . I'll get one."

"You want me to look around?" Brandon said.

"If you want," Deetz said, getting a cup and tea bag for Kristen. "But I've been over it. Everywhere. Mom's going to need to look when she gets here."

Kristen shot Brandon a flash of her eyes as if to say how creepy the whole thing was.

The garage door could be heard going up.

"That's Mom." Brandon stood and went to the door leading to the garage.

Deetz served Kristen her cup of tea. He'd already texted Joanie and the family telling them he had not noticed anything missing or destroyed.

"Thank you so much," Kristen said. "And thank you again for a wonderful wedding. It was beautiful. You guys really went all out."

Leena blew into the house first. "We've got a carload full of wedding gifts," she announced. "And J.P. and Tammy are right behind us with another carload full. You guys made bank." She leaned on the island next to Kristen and said, "I thought you love-birds would be long gone by now."

Kristen laughed and gave Leena a hug. "We wanted to stop by here first. We'll be going soon."

"Well Dad, what's the damage?" Leena said, opening the fridge and searching around, still wearing her big winter coat.

Brandon came back in from the garage with his arm around his mom. He was some eight inches taller than petite Joanie. He helped her get her coat off as Deetz gave her a kiss, and Kristen greeted her with a hug. Leena took her own coat off, too.

"Well, what's the damage?" Joanie said.

They all laughed.

"Mom, I just said those exact words!" Leena said. "That old saying must be true, that the bad apple doesn't fall far from the tree!"

Laughter filled the room again. As long as Brandon could remember, Leena had always been the one to crack everyone up. Considering her high-functioning autism, she was probably smarter than Brandon and J.P. put together. Comments like the "bad" apple were classic coming from Leena. She often had no filter and actually said what everyone else was thinking but was too afraid to say.

Between the festive wedding, the frigid weather, and the aura of Christmas, an unspoken joy filled the room, a sweet moment of love and laughter Deetz hoped he would always remember.

To top it off, J.P. and Tammy came blowing in through the garage next.

They all hugged and greeted one another there in the cozy kitchen.

Joanie said, "I hope we have something stronger than tea!"

Deetz fetched several bottles of wine from the rack and J.P. volunteered to open them.

Once everyone who wanted it had a glass, they congregated in the foyer where Deetz showed everyone the splintered door. He told those who hadn't heard about the mysterious jug of milk and glass, and explained that the forensics team had come up with nothing.

"This is precisely why we need a security camera, Wayne," said Joanie.

Deetz shook his head and held up a hand. "Believe me, I know. Everyone here has told me that. I'll get one, I promise. You're like the tenth person . . ."

Joanie headed toward the master bedroom. "I'm going to check my jewelry box. Leena, you should check your room, honey."

Leena headed for the stairs. "Will do, Mom. This is where I put my investigative savvy to work."

"Oh, hey, dear—I didn't tell you, Brodie came over," Deetz called.

Joanie peeked her head back out of the doorway leading to the bedroom. "What did he say?"

"Just that he saw a dark van backed in close to the garage. He didn't see anything else."

"He didn't see anyone?"

"Huh-uh. He saw the van on his way home from getting a pizza. He knew we had the wedding, so he called 911, and then he just forgot about it."

Joanie sighed and turned back into the bedroom.

"He said they got a gift for the newlyweds," Deetz called, then looked at Brandon and Kristen. "He said he'll bring it by soon."

"That was nice of them," Kristen said. "I don't think I've ever met them."

"I'm going to check my room. You want to come?" Brandon said to Kristen.

"I'll pass on that. This dress and those steps aren't a good combination."

Brandon got upstairs and ducked his head into Leena's room. "Everything okay?"

Leena spun around. "Oh my gosh! Are you trying to give me a heart attack?"

He laughed. "Sorry, Sis."

"Just like old times. A knock or heads-up would be good next time. To answer your question, I don't see one single thing out of place. Not the tiniest thing. I don't think they came in here."

"Good." Brandon went off to check his old bedroom.

DEETZ, Kristen, J.P., and Tammy had returned to the kitchen when Joanie called for Wayne to come into their bedroom.

Deetz didn't like the sound of her voice or the fact she was calling him in there alone.

His heart rate kicked up as he entered the bedroom.

"What is it?"

Joanie's face was flushed. She paced next to her dresser with her arms crossed, chewing at the cuticle of a thumb. Two of her dresser drawers were open. Deetz hadn't looked in her clothes drawers.

Joanie spoke quietly, almost in a whisper. "My underwear's gone. All of it." She threw a hand toward the drawers.

Deetz approached, squeezed her arm, and looked down at the drawers.

They were completely empty.

"You mean like bras and panties and that kind of thing?" he said, his face red.

She nodded, crossed her arms again, and paced.

"What else? Jewelry?"

"It's all there, I think."

Deetz headed for the walk-in closet. "Have you checked your clothes in here?"

She followed him in.

"Have you?" His heart pounded.

"No." She began to shuffle through her clothes on hangers, fast, one by one. Then she stopped and examined all of them. "I think everything's here."

"What about shoes?"

She stuck her hands on her waist and tilted her head. "Really, Wayne?"

"Just check, please. If he took bras and panties, who knows?"

Joanie dropped to one knee and scanned the many pairs of shoes.

Deetz walked back out to their sinks and leaned against the counter, wracking his brain to figure out who would do this.

"My gold high heels are gone," Joanie stared up at him from the closet. "The really high heels."

7

———

It was a bright, cold Monday morning and Joanie was upstairs in Brandon's old bedroom, shoving boxes from Target and Amazon around, stacking them, and trying to find a place for all of the wedding gifts people had brought. She was feeling a great sense of relief that the festivities were over and that Brandon and Kristen had made it safely to their hotel on Hawaii's Big Island, Mauna Lani.

When they returned in a week, the newlyweds would move into a new apartment in the same complex where Brandon and Clarence had shared a place, near downtown Portland. Clarence had found a roommate to replace Brandon, a young man currently going through the police academy, and Brandon and Kristen would be moving to a unit just down the hallway. Joanie loved Clarence and was glad he and Brandon would still be close; they were good for each other.

She shook her head in disbelief, recalling how Randall Trent had barged into the wedding ceremony late and made a scene at the reception. He'd been so drunk by the time it ended that he spun around, accidentally shattered a glass, and fell flat on his face right in the middle of the send-off for Brandon and Kristen. When Roxanne had tried to help him up, she practically came out of her dress and almost fell down herself.

It was difficult not to care about what their friends must have thought. Joanie's cheeks got warm just thinking about how embarrassing it had been. She was thankful Wayne hadn't been there for that part of it. She smiled and shrugged. There was really nothing they could have done about Randall showing up—he was Roxanne's responsibility.

It did nag at Joanie that Roxanne had been in contact with Randall, and that he may have even been staying with her prior to the wedding; that was what people were saying. For all Joanie knew, Roxanne may have told Randall to just show up at the wedding without being invited. Joanie could only hope that Randall had moved on and out of their lives. And she prayed for Kristen, that she would be healthy and happy and that she would bring out the best in Brandon in the weeks, months, and years ahead.

Joanie sat on the only space available at the end of Brandon's bed and absorbed the silence. She was glad Leena was at work. She was so proud of that girl. And today was the day Wayne was due to start training his replacement, some guy who'd just gotten a divorce and was moving to Portland from Seattle to "start over."

God, how she longed for the end of the month when Wayne would be done with police work for good. She did the math in her head. Eighteen more days and he would be officially retired. The job —and all that had come with it—had taken its toll on their family.

She wondered if the break-in had anything to do with Wayne's work. He'd put many vicious people away during his thirty five years of police service. He'd received death threats. Leena had even been kidnapped by an accomplice of the infamous Portland shooter, Rogan Sneed, who was spending multiple life sentences in prison.

She thought she heard something downstairs.

She sat very still, listening.

Could they be back?

After some twenty seconds she determined it had just been the wind.

The reality that someone had roamed through their house, invaded their privacy, and stolen her private things—was eerie. What would they do with her things? What were their motives? Why risk breaking into the home of a veteran police investigator?

Or, she supposed, it could have been random. Maybe the intruder knew nothing about them. Maybe he was just some nutcase or drug fiend who chose their house randomly. But if that were the case, why had he not taken anything of value?

The doorbell rang.

Joanie's heart raced.

She zig-zagged through the boxes and made her way to the window. There were no cars in the driveway below. From that vantage point she couldn't see who was at the front door. *Another good reason to have a security camera, Wayne!*

She went to the stairs and could see through the small window at the door on her way down that it was Brodie Enoch, standing there in his winter coat and hat, holding a white box with a gold bow. She hoped Jeanette was with him, or it would be completely awkward.

She got to the landing and peeked out—no Jeanette.

Ugh.

She pulled the door open.

"Greetings," Brodie said, bouncing on his toes.

"Hello. Oh, wow, what's this?" Joanie said.

"As promised." Brodie lifted the box, which was about a foot in diameter and appeared heavy in his arms. "A gift for the newly-weds." His left eye twitched repeatedly.

"Oh, how kind of you." Joanie reached out to take the box.

"No." Brodie shook his head. "I insist. Let me take it in for you. It's quite heavy."

"Oh . . . okay." Reluctantly, she opened the door further and stepped inside.

He came in behind her, the cold air sweeping in with him. "Where would you like it?"

"Right here is fine." She pointed to the wood floor right there in the foyer.

"Are you sure? I can take it anywhere for you." He held it so it rested atop his right thigh. "Do you have someplace where you're keeping all their gifts?"

Hmm. That seemed quite insightful for a man. Joanie knew the Enochs had two adult children, both married, and guessed they'd been through it before.

"We did that for Blake and his wife." Brodie's mouth twitched several times, like two quick smiles in fast motion. "Our dining room was packed with their stuff for weeks."

Joanie snapped out of it and again pointed to the foyer floor. "This is fine, really. Wayne can take it from here."

"Whatever you say, my lady."

My lady?

Brodie bent over and set the box on the floor, then straightened and set his shoulders back with a stretch and a sigh. "Sorry about the other night, the break-in. Too bad."

"Oh," she shook her head and found herself at a loss for how to respond. "Yeah . . . odd timing with the wedding and all."

"I'll say. Too bad Wayne had to miss some of the reception."

"I know. It was."

"When I came by that night, they hadn't found much of anything disturbed." He blinked involuntarily in rapid succession. "That was good, I guess . . ."

"Yeah, yeah . . . As good as it could be for a break-in, I suppose."

He crossed his arms. "So, they didn't take anything at all?"

He looked so intently into her eyes that it took her breath away for a moment.

She felt almost violated.

Her face flushed.

She shook her head slightly, not about to tell him what they'd taken. "Huh uh . . . no, not that we can tell."

"Huh." He frowned so much that the corners of his mouth curled down to his chin, and he continued to stare at her, as if examining her, waiting for more.

She felt so uneasy.

"What do the police make of it?" he said

"Well . . ." Joanie wanted him gone. She took steps toward the front door in hopes that he would follow, but he didn't budge. "They dusted for prints, of course," she said. "We're still waiting on the results." She wasn't sure why she lied. She just didn't want to divulge any information to him.

"Jeanette would be beside herself if that happened to us," he said. "She wouldn't sleep, knowing someone had been in our house —doing who knows what?"

Why are you even saying this?

Was he trying to freak her out? What response did he want?

Joanie finished walking to the door and turned around to face him.

He still hadn't moved the five feet he needed to in order to leave.

"Sorry to rush you off," she said. "I've got a million things going on today."

Her hands trembled and she moved her feet nervously.

Brodie's head dropped back and he laughed, his pronounced Adam's apple bulging.

He meandered to the door loosely, his long arms dangling, as if in slow motion.

"Thank you again for the gift." Joanie pushed the door open and held it for him. "I'm sure they'll love it."

"Oh, it's our pleasure. I hope so." Twitch, twitch. "It's both practical and a bit laughable—wink, wink."

He chuckled and passed by her uncomfortably close; much closer than he had to.

That's when she smelled it.

Dante's Dance.

The cologne Wayne wore.

She could barely breathe.

"Bye now," she managed. Her head spun as she pushed the heavy front door closed while Brodie was still saying goodbye.

She peeked out to make sure he was headed back to his house and then rushed into the master bedroom.

White stars spun in her vision as she raced through the bedroom to the bathroom.

One glance at Wayne's sink and she heard herself yelp.

She stopped cold.

Two bottles of cologne always sat there.

One remained there now.

Dante's Dance was gone.

8

———————

Deetz was infuriated. He sat at a small conference room table at the Portland Police precinct, impatiently waiting for the new guy to show up. He looked at his watch again. Howard Googan, his replacement, was exactly twelve minutes late. Deetz stood and walked out to the hallway, thinking perhaps Googan was lost, but there was no sign of the man.

Just as Deetz walked back into the conference room, he heard Sergeant Tidwell call his name. Deetz reversed direction and met Tidwell in the hallway.

Tidwell patted Deetz on the back with a legal pad. "Let's go in here for a minute."

"Googan's late," Deetz said, as he walked back into the conference room.

"How late?" Tidwell said.

Deetz looked at his watch again. "Thirteen minutes."

Tidwell chuckled. "He'll be here." He turned toward Deetz and crossed his arms with the pad in one hand.

"I told you I wasn't high on the guy," Deetz said. "His first day and he's late."

Tidwell nodded sarcastically, apparently not worried one bit that the "seasoned pro" from Seattle was tardy on his first day of work.

"Do you want to know what I found out about Brandon's father-in-law, or not?" Tidwell said.

That got Deetz's attention.

"Randall Trent? Shoot, yeah. What'd you find?"

Tidwell uncrossed his arms, put on his reading glasses, and adjusted the pad at reading distance. "Randall Trent, fifty-seven, a.k.a. Roderick Farmer, Bart Sanders, and Walter Mason. Once served nine months in Washington State Penitentiary for elder fraud." Tidwell glanced up at Deetz, whose eyes were huge, then back at the pad. "Working as all three aliases at various times, Trent impersonated employees from the IRS, Medicare, and the Social Security Administration, in order to gain their trust, create a sense of urgency, glean personal information, and, ultimately, collect various forms of bogus payments. He pulled off his schemes using phone calls, emails, text messages, social media, and in-person visits."

"No - way," Deetz said, feeling light-headed.

Tidwell looked at him. "The guy's a conman to the nth degree, Wayne. That's how he's made his living." Tidwell looked back at his pad. "He's done small stints in and out of prison ever since he was nineteen. Tech support scams, impersonation, investment fraud, home repair scams, and sweepstakes cons."

All Deetz could think about was that Randall was Kristen's bloodline, her lineage. That may well have contributed to her mental challenges. And now she was pregnant with Brandon's child.

"I don't think the guy has worked an honest job in his life," Tidwell continued. "It looks like he sets up shop someplace, in some small- to mid-size community, he does these scams—some local, some not—and then, for whatever reason, he pulls up stakes and moves on to the next town. This says he's lived in Montana, Utah, Nevada, and Northern California. A real drifter."

"Is he wanted anywhere now?"

"Negative. If I had to guess I'd say he's between stops."

"Why did he show up here, now?"

"Good question." Tidwell handed Deetz the notepad and headed for the door. "Welcome to the family." As he disappeared around the corner he yelled, "Don't be too hard on the new guy."

Deetz contemplated confronting Randall—or whatever his name

was—just to tell him what he knew. But why? What good would that do anyone?

He would need to tell Brandon and Kristen, and perhaps Roxanne, if she didn't already know about Randall's sordid past.

A quick knock at the door.

"Morning," grunted Howard Googan, who came in bundled up in a big wool hat and coat, cup of coffee in one hand, and a backpack over his shoulder.

So, buying coffee was more important than being on time for his first day of work?

Deetz looked at his watch. "Good morning. Do you realize you're twenty minutes late?"

Googan sat with a huff. "I didn't know what to expect with the traffic. It's worse than Seattle."

"But you found time to get your coffee."

"Okay, you made your point. We're both veterans. Are we really going to start off on the wrong foot like this?"

The gall of this guy.

"I'd rather not, but you're twenty minutes late on your first day," Deetz said. "Put yourself in my shoes. You're right, I'm a veteran. I've put in my thirty-five years right here with the PPB. Do I deserve to sit around waiting on a new employee? You need to be on time or early from now on."

Googan closed his eyes, frowned, shook his head, and made a barely audible groan, then sipped his coffee.

"Can I count on you to be on time from now on?" Deetz said. "I think we all know how to plan around traffic."

"Is this a pride thing, or what?" Googan said, with a brief laugh. "I've been at this as long as you. Do we really need to argue about a few minutes? Like I said, we're both professionals. Let's act like it."

Deetz stood very still and stared at him, thinking of a hundred different ways he could blast the guy.

Patience. Your days here are almost done.

After another moment, Deetz said, "Look, I've got about two weeks to train you. I'm not going to sit around and wait for you to show up when we're supposed to meet. You need to be on time—or you'll be out of a job."

"But the thing is, you're not my boss."

Deetz was shocked.

He could not believe the nerve of this guy.

"You know what? For the next two weeks, I *am* your boss and—"

"I work for Sergeant Tidwell. He hired me."

"Against my advice, I'll have you know!" Deetz instantly regretted the outburst. It was unprofessional and immature. He felt slightly dizzy from the anger boiling inside him. "Look, Googan, I'm not going to stand here and argue with you. My job is to teach you what I do in this role, to get you ready for when I leave."

"I'm sure I could just about do it now."

Deetz's face burned and his eyes shot lasers into the overweight, arrogant man seated in the chair five feet from him. He could not believe the nerve of this guy.

"Sergeant Tidwell did tell you I'd be training you, correct?"

"He said you were on your way out to pasture and you'd be doing time for a few more weeks, then the gig would be mine. You do know I've done this job before, right?"

"Not here, you haven't."

Googan shrugged. "An investigator's an investigator."

"You know what?" Deetz was just about to go vent to Tidwell when his phone buzzed. He got it out and examined the screen. It was a text from Joanie:

> I need to talk to you right now if you can!

It was unlike Joanie to ask Deetz to call her during work.

Joanie took immediate priority.

Deetz leaned over to his stuff on the table and grabbed the top sheet of paper listing the items he planned to cover that day with Googan, as well as a manilla folder containing information about a Portland woman who'd gone missing several days earlier. He tossed the items in front of Googan. "Look these things over. I'll be right back."

Googan said nothing as Deetz left the room and called Joanie.

She picked up on the first ring.

"Hey," she said. "Sorry to bother you, but I need to ask you something."

Her voice sounded panicked and that instantly made him uneasy.

"Okay, what's up?" he said, unconsciously holding his breath.

"Do you know where your *Dante's Dance* is?"

He didn't even have to think about it. "By my sink. Why?"

"It's not there," Joanie blurted. "I think whoever broke in took it."

"No," Deetz said. "I must've put it in a drawer without thinking."

"I've looked. It's not anywhere," Joanie said with growing concern in her voice.

"I'll look when I get home, honey. Don't worry about it. Why are you looking for it? What made you get onto this?"

"You're going to think I'm crazy."

"Okay . . ."

"Brodie Enoch brought over a gift for Brandon and Kristen. He's just weird, by the way."

It figured Brodie would wait until Deetz was gone to pay a visit.

"When he was leaving, I smelled *Dante's Dance* on him."

9

———

THAT EVENING, Joanie made a salad in the kitchen while her lasagna baked in the oven. She was a bit nervous because they'd invited Roxanne for dinner at the last minute. They did so for two reasons—to extend her courtesy in order to keep their relationship positive since she was now family, and to feel her out on what she knew about Randall Trent's dark past, thinking perhaps she may need to be warned.

Wayne was busy installing a security camera at the front exterior entryway of their house, just above the front door. It was dark and freezing outside with a slight drizzle in the air. He was in and out fetching the various tools he needed. Joanie had already reprimanded him several times for letting all the cold air in when they were about to have a guest. Wayne wore a winter parka and hat, gloves on and off, and he had a headlamp strapped to his head to help him see his project in the low light.

When he had arrived home from work the first thing he and Joanie had done was search for the missing bottle of cologne, but they didn't find it. She filled him in on Brodie's odd visit. Wayne took the gift box up to Brandon's old bedroom. Then they'd gone their separate ways—him to his project, her to make dinner— agreeing to talk more about the whole thing later.

While Wayne was on the ladder hovering above the front door, penciling where he would drill holes to anchor the brace for the

45

camera, his mind kept going back to the break-in—the milk, Joanie's missing underwear and shoes, and now his bottle of cologne. Whoever broke in could have taken computers, TVs, jewelry, and other valuables, but they weren't interested. No, this was someone playing head games with them.

It could be any number of perverts Deetz had busted over the years, but he'd already shuffled through the worst of those and none of them had been deeply personal cases or would have left much reason for this kind of twisted vengeance.

They didn't know Brodie and Jeanette Enoch very well at all.

Brodie was an outdoorsman who enjoyed camping, hiking, rock climbing, and that sort of thing. Deetz recalled him saying something about having a camper at one time, but there wasn't one at their house next door. So he was thinking they'd sold it or they kept it parked somewhere else. Brodie worked remotely from his home in logistics for a big cell phone company, arranging where they would place temporary cell towers after big storms and natural disasters around the world.

Jeanette was extremely shy. She reminded Deetz of the old homesteaders, often wearing long denim skirts, tennis shoes, and very modest clothing. She often wore a mask—inside, outside, in the car, wherever. Deetz recalled Brodie joking once that Jeanette had received every vaccine known to man. She was extremely thin and pale. She had homeschooled their kids all the way through high school. Now, Deetz didn't know what she did; he barely ever saw her. When he did, she would look away quickly and go into the house, pretending she hadn't seen him.

Headlights lit up the front entryway. Deetz turned to look and saw that a car had pulled in the driveway and was facing him now. He looked at his watch. Roxanne wasn't due for another twenty minutes, but he had a hunch it was her.

Deetz continued what he was doing and noticed the headlights went out.

He heard a car door open.

"I hope I'm not too early." It was Roxanne.

Ugh. He'd hoped to get the camera finished before she arrived.

"Hey Roxanne," Deetz called. "Come in."

Deetz got down from the ladder, welcomed Roxanne at the front door, and showed her into the house. Joanie was as surprised as Deetz to see their guest so early. He took her coat, hung it in the hall closet, and assured Joanie that he would only be a few more minutes.

BY THE TIME Deetz got finished installing the security camera and the accompanying app on his phone, Joanie and Roxanne were seated at the dinner table in the warm kitchen, sipping Chianti and munching on a bowl of mixed nuts. He poured a glass and joined them.

"Roxanne, show Wayne the picture from Kristen," Joanie said.

Roxanne worked her phone for a few seconds and handed it to Deetz.

"Fancy dinner out last night," Roxanne said.

It was a honeymoon picture of Kristen and Brandon all dressed up at a formal candlelit dinner in a cozy restaurant. Their waiter must have taken it.

"They sure do look happy," Deetz said, handing the phone back.

Roxanne looked at the photo again. "Not a care in the world. That Brandon is so handsome. My Lord, they are a good-looking couple, aren't they?"

"Brandon said they went out on a catamaran today," Deetz said.

"And they're going zip-lining, too," Joanie added.

"My, my." Roxanne shook her head and put her phone away. "I can't imagine. I've never been anyplace."

"Really?" Joanie said. "You never traveled much?"

"Much! I've never been on an airplane! My parents were poor as dirt. Never went to college. Couldn't afford it. Then I fell in with Randall. Well, you can imagine how that went. You got a good taste of what he's like at the wedding. But, honestly, he's not like that. Only when he drinks. He's really just a big cuddly teddy bear."

Joanie and Wayne were speechless and waited to see if she would continue.

"I never told Kristen, but he has called me on and off over the years." Roxanne took a quick sip of her wine, leaving lipstick around the rim of the glass. "He'd be in one fix or another. Usually needing money. I've been civil to him. Course, I told him Kristen was getting married. Well, wouldn't you know, he showed up on my doorstep Thursday before. I pleaded with him not to come. He said he wouldn't . . . I hope he wasn't too much of an embarrassment to you and your family—and all the guests."

Deetz and Joanie glanced at each other awkwardly, unsure who would speak up first.

"Oh, it . . . we took everything in stride," Joanie said.

"I know you did," Roxanne said. "Everyone was gracious. I even had a bit too much to drink myself. It was quite a night to remember—what I can of it." She laughed at her own joke.

"Is Randall still staying with you?" Deetz said.

Joanie shot him a mean look and shook her head.

"He is . . . but it's nothing . . . I mean, we're not having relations or anything like that."

Joanie rolled her eyes at him.

"Oh, I didn't mean to imply that. Sorry," Deetz said. "It's just that, well, after the wedding I did some checking on Randall in our police database—"

"Oh boy, here it comes," Roxanne said, pushing her chair back a few inches.

"I just don't want him to be a danger to you, or a threat of any kind," Deetz said.

Roxanne waved a hand. "He's harmless. I'm strong. He knows it. He ain't gonna pull any of his shenanigans on me. Why? What'd you find?"

"So, you know he's done time in prison—"

Joanie slowly stood up. "Dinner's just about ready. Wayne, can you do refills before we say grace."

"Sure." He stood.

"I know about that," Roxanne said. "He claims he was framed, that they got the wrong man."

"Do you know what he did time for?" Deetz said, crossing to get the bottle of wine and a pitcher of water.

Joanie glared at him about how uncomfortable the whole thing was getting.

"All I know is it had something to do with a check that was . . . cashed illegally or something like that."

"Roxanne, Randall is a scammer," Deetz said. "He swindles

elderly people out of their life savings. He's done so in one way or another most of his adult life. I need for you to know the truth. I'm sorry."

Roxanne blinked and looked at Joanie, who just stared at her across the room with a look of compassion.

Deetz continued. "He lies to old people about losing their social security benefits, about home repairs and investments. He scares them, then he talks them into giving him their personal information in order to scam them out of as much money as he can get."

Roxanne was shaking her head. "I don't believe you. No. I can't. Randall wouldn't do that."

Joanie stepped toward her. "Wayne doesn't want anything to happen to you, Roxanne. We thought you should know the truth; in case you didn't already."

Roxanne continued to shake her head as she looked down and fidgeted with her fingers. "I think I better go," she finally said, and started to get up.

Deetz stood and put a hand on her shoulder. "Please don't. We invited you to have dinner with us. We're family now. Stay and eat. We're on your side. We'll drop this now and move onto other things."

She gave a small smile to Deetz and turned to Joanie. "I'm so embarrassed."

"Why should you be embarrassed?" Joanie said. "You're working two jobs to make ends meet. You raised Kristen and look at her now."

"She has her issues. Sometimes I think she may be, what do they call it, polarized?"

"Bi-polar?" Deetz said.

Roxanne nodded. "Yes, bi-polar. Mood swings. Fits of jealously."

Joanie glanced at Wayne with a look of concern. "Well," she said, "we all have issues."

"We want to support you, Roxanne. We thought it was critical that you know the truth about Randall," Deetz said.

"Come on," Joanie said. "This lasagna's hot. My bread is ready. We're all set. Wayne, why don't you bless it."

"I can't. Would you get my coat, Wayne?" Roxanne said. "This is going to bother me to no end. I'm sorry. You're both so nice for inviting me—and for watching out for me."

"But you have to eat, Roxanne," said Joanie.

"I can't think about food right now. I need to get home. Deal with this."

Wayne showed up with her coat and helped her get it on.

"I'm more embarrassed than ever now," she said, heading toward the foyer. "Forgive me for all the trouble."

And with that, she was gone, into the freezing night.

10

Randall was kicked back in the blue recliner at Roxanne's place that evening with a bag of Ranch-flavored Doritos in his lap, a can of Budweiser making rings on the small table next to him, and an episode of Hoarders blaring from the glowing TV, the only light in the small house.

He heard the door slam shut and wondered what Roxanne would be doing home already. She was supposed to be having dinner with the cop and his wife.

Roxanne entered the kitchen without saying anything—probably because the TV was so loud—turned on the light above the stove and set a large McDonald's bag on the counter.

He dug the remote out of the crack in the chair with a grunt and muted the TV.

They looked at each other from twenty-five feet apart.

"Well?" he said. "What are you doing back so early and why the Mickey D's? What happened?"

She stopped getting the hamburgers and fries out of the bag, set both hands on the counter, and stared at him. "They know everything about you." She nodded her head repeatedly as if to say, 'I told you so.' "The whole kit and caboodle. The whole nine yards. And some of it's worse than you told me."

"How?" He brought the chair upright and glared at her. "How'd they find out?"

"He's a police investigator, Randall! After the way you behaved at the wedding, he put your name in one of those big police computers. My Lord, he read me a rap sheet a mile long."

Randall cursed and scrunched up the bag of Doritos, grabbed his beer, and, with great effort, got to his feet. He had on his usual nighttime attire, gray sweatpants and sweatshirt, and white socks that had been worn too many nights.

"How'd that even come up?" he said, setting the Doritos and beer on the counter, then burping.

"How would it *not* come up, Randall? That's the reason they had me over—to tell me about your sordid past. To *warn* me. They thought they were doing me a big favor."

"Hmm." He squeezed his jaw with a pudgy hand. "They didn't suspect *you*, did they?"

"No, no, no, no."

"Well, that's good."

"Yes, Randall, but we need to shut it down. I told you, I'm not getting caught. I wouldn't last a day in prison."

"We can't stop now, Roxy. We're right in the middle of this thing. You know that. We've got like two or three widows who are about to spill."

"Not only are we stopping, but you need to leave. I can't have you here. It's raising too many suspicions. I've got my name to think about. Besides, it all makes me feel dirty. It's not right."

He just stared at her.

"I live in this town. You don't," she said. "I'm here year-round, every day. People talk."

"Okay. I get it. I understand. But will you just work with me for one more week? After that, I'm out of here. Please, Roxy. I need the money."

"No, Randall. I told you—I'm done. And you need to go."

Suddenly, he reached over and squeezed her wrist so hard that his face contorted into what looked like the mask of a devil. "You'll do what I say or I'll tell Deetz of your involvement. Your new family will love that."

"How much have you had to drink? That's your problem. You get like this every time you drink too much. Can you just be happy with one beer? You have one, you have eight."

"I mean it," he seethed. "I'll tell them. And where will that leave you?"

He squeezed her wrist even harder.

"Ouch!" She cried and cursed. "Okay. But one week and you're gone. And if not, I swear I'll call the police."

He threw her wrist free.

"I want you out before Kristen and Brandon get back from the honeymoon," Roxanne said, digging in her coat pocket for her vape pen.

Randall ignored her and opened one of the hamburgers she had set out.

She exhaled a thick, huge cloud of smoke.

He cussed. "That's disgusting. I'm trying to eat here."

She shook her head, wrestled off her winter coat, and hung it on one of the crowded hooks on the wall.

He fetched a tray from a cupboard, piled it with food, and headed back to his chair.

"We need to call that Jensen lady—tonight," he said.

Roxanne, who had taken a mouthful of hamburger, stared at him. "You mean I do."

"Yes, and I need to be there for backup. I'm the supervisor, remember?"

She picked up some fries, dipped them in ketchup, and stuffed them into her mouth.

"Hear me?" he yelled.

She glared at him and nodded.

"Nighttime's the best time," he said. "And she's ready to crack."

Roxanne got a plastic jug of milk out of the fridge and poured a glass. "Look, I'm beat, so if we're going to do it, we need to do it soon. I'm ready for some shut eye."

"Let me finish eating and go to the toilet, then we'll hit it."

THEY MET thirty minutes later in the small spare room upstairs that Randall had set up as his temporary work headquarters. Two chairs and card tables were set up side-by-side. On them sat a cheap black metal lamp, the light from which shone beside a large desktop computer, a laptop computer, and various pads, pens, calculators, notes, and pencils.

Randall and Roxanne sat next to each other on the folding chairs. Both wore headsets with microphones. He was at the desktop; she was on the laptop.

He pointed at some notes he'd taken last time. "Remember, her husband died about three months ago. His name was Henry. He had lymphoma. The story is, he had a life insurance policy—"

"Stop, Randall. I know. I remember. Let's just make the call. I'm so tired I can't even think straight."

"Okay, then, here we go. Check, check, check, check. Can you hear me?"

She nodded.

"Respond verbally," he hissed.

"I copy you!" she spat back.

He used a burner phone to dial the number.

It rang five times before a weak, female voice said, "Hello."

"Good evening, is this Mrs. Jensen?" Roxanne said.

"Yes, it is. Who's calling?"

"Ma'am, this is Dorothy Chievers with Modern Mutual Life Insurance company in Springfield, Missouri. Do you remember me?"

There was a pause. "Yes, I believe so."

"If you'll recall, we were notified of your husband Henry's death. He had a sizable life insurance policy with us, and we need to get a bit more information from you before we can cut you the check. I believe we were interrupted last time we talked—you had to leave because someone had arrived to take you to run errands."

There was a long pause. "I told the man from your company I wasn't aware Henry had a policy with you."

"Yes, I remember. I was on that call with him." Roxanne eyed Randall then looked at her notes. "He's my supervisor, Roderick Farmer. He is not on the call with me tonight, but he has authorized me to cut you this check. All I need is for you to confirm your date and place of birth, social security number, and a few more things." She scanned the pad in front of her. "You've already given me your full name, current address, the name of your bank, and your driver's license number."

"I don't know about this," said Mrs. Jensen. "I've read a lot lately about these scammers." Her voice trailed off.

The line went silent.

Roxanne's head cranked toward Randall.

He whirled his hand in a circle repeatedly and whispered for Roxanne to keep on script.

"As I mentioned, Mrs. Jensen, we are in Missouri, so we can't do this in person. If you'll just give me your social security number, we'll cut you that check for, let me see here, three hundred and seventy-five thousand dollars. Your husband was a smart man to have this policy. He was thinking ahead to this very day. He must have loved you very much."

Randall rolled his eyes.

Mrs. Jensen could be heard sniffling, perhaps even shedding a tear. After a moment, she said, "Why Missouri, though? I live in Portland, Oregon."

Mrs. Jensen was one of many unsuspecting people whose private information Roxanne had stolen on her job at the Cornerstop Café.

"Oh, Modern Mutual is a national company. International, in fact," Roxanne lied. "Your husband was a wise cookie. He knew a good straight term life insurance policy when he saw one. Low premium, high benefit."

"But I've already been notified about a life insurance benefit from State Trust."

Roxanne's dark eyes flicked toward Randall.

"Yes. Henry mentioned when he got this policy that he already had another one with State Trust. This one was such a good deal, he said he couldn't pass it up. He told us he had a feeling you would outlive him, and he just wanted to be extra sure you had enough money to be totally covered and comfortable if and when he passed."

"God love him," Mrs. Jensen mumbled. "What is it you need from me again?"

11

———

It was midday Thursday—cold, gray, and raining. Joanie Deetz normally didn't go into the city to the ritzy Portland Plaza of Shoppes, a high-end, boutique mall shimmering with steel, glass, dark wood, skylights, and glossy marble floors. But she'd promised Brandon and Kristen that while they were gone, she would return a wedding gift to a fancy shop in the complex.

Between the nasty weather, the crowded parking lot full of cars belonging to Christmas shoppers, and the heavy box she was returning (a huge pottery bowl), Joanie decided to use the valet parking service so she could dash in and out under cover.

After stopping at a kiosk to examine a glowing map of the mall, she found the location of the store and headed in that direction. The stores along the way were magnificent, packed with the finest clothing, shoes, home décor, and jewelry—and all decorated for Christmas in rich reds and greens, and shiny silver and gold.

The distinct smell of grilled meat filled her senses, and she came to an intimate restaurant that featured thick white wood shutters, open to the mall, plush red carpet, and cozy private booths of cushy white leather. Festive ivy interlaced with glass ornaments was draped over the wood shutters. A huge fire blazed in the large stone fireplace. The waiters wore starched white shirts and black slacks and shoes.

Most of the patrons sat close over candlelit tables, sipping cock-

56

tails, and probably discussing what was in the shopping bags that surrounded them, and what more they needed to buy for those on their Christmas lists.

Joanie wished she was seated at one of the booths with Wayne. It was so romantic.

In the next booth she looked at, she saw familiar faces.

She slowed her pace.

Oh my gosh!

It was Brodie Enoch and . . .

Joanie practically stopped walking.

Brodie's wife, Jeanette, sat across from him, but she looked nothing like her homely self. She wore no mask and her hair was shiny and even highlighted. She wore makeup. She resembled a fashion model, torn from the pages of a magazine. The shimmery red dress she wore . . .

Joanie almost dropped the heavy box.

Jeanette's red dress looked *exactly* like one of Joanie's dresses.

Alarms blared in Joanie's head as her focus shifted down to Jeanette's feet . . . gold high-heels! They were Joanie's! The ones that had been stolen during the break-in.

No . . .

They mustn't see her.

Joanie took one last look—took a picture of the scene in her mind—and began walking, fast, away from the restaurant.

Two stores down she found a bench and stopped.

She set the box down.

Feeling dizzy, she sat, her mind blown.

Her hand was on her forehead.

She was hot and sweaty and light-headed.

She couldn't have just seen what she thought she saw.

Her neighbors, Brodie and Jeanette Enoch. Jeanette, wearing the shoes that had been stolen. And one of Joanie's dresses, too? It must've been stolen and Joanie hadn't noticed.

Brodie in coat and tie.

Jeanette, who normally looked like a modest pioneer woman, looked more like a chic runway model. She was probably wearing Joanie's things underneath.

Sick!

Joanie's hands trembled uncontrollably as she opened her purse and searched for her phone and, at the same time, kept looking up to make sure the Enochs weren't coming. She couldn't remember seeing what stage of the meal they were in.

Maybe Joanie was mistaken. Maybe those weren't her shoes and Jeanette simply owned the same red dress. It was possible.

She took a deep breath and dialed Wayne.

"Hey, honey," he answered.

"You're not going to believe this." As fast as she could, she explained what she'd just seen.

There was a long pause.

"Are you *sure* it's them? That's a long way from home," Wayne said.

"Yes. It's them! I've never seen her look like this. Wayne, *they did it*. They broke into our house!"

"Don't let them see you. Where are you now?"

She explained where she was and that she still had to make the return.

"Look, for now all you can do is finish your errand and get out of there. Then, check for the red dress when you get home."

"I hope I'm wrong. I've *got* to be wrong."

"I hope you're wrong, too," he said.

She looked at the heavy box, then up to where she had to go, then back toward the restaurant.

"Honey?" Wayne said. "What's happening?"

"Nothing. I'm just . . . I'm . . . this blows my mind."

"We'll talk about it together, okay? For now, make the return and go home. That's all you can do right now. We'll figure it all out. Try not to worry about it."

"Wayne, they're our neighbors. If they went into our house—"

"I know. I know. It's beyond weird. But let's make sure first."

She took a deep breath, paused, and resolved to calm herself.

"God, please just get Joanie home safely and protect us," Deetz prayed.

"Yes, Lord."

"You okay?" Wayne said.

"Yeah." She still felt light-headed. "I'll be okay."

"You sure?"

"Yeah." She took a deep breath and exhaled aloud. "We've got to get to the bottom of this," she said, her heart still pounding.

"We will, we will. For now, just do the return and get home. Check on the red dress and let me know."

"Okay, okay. I'll talk to you later."

She dropped the phone in her bag, got up, and glanced one last time in the direction of the restaurant. Not seeing the Enochs, she lugged the box off the bench and headed off to make the return.

JOANIE WAS ONLY able to get store credit for the bowl, and she wasn't going to stand there and argue. She tucked the gift card in her wallet with trembling hands, slipped the wallet in her purse, and turned to leave the store. She zig-zagged quickly past plush couches and chairs, pillows and candles, lamps and coffee tables.

As she exited the store back into the mall the way she had come, her mind buzzed with questions and confusion about the red dress, the gold shoes, and the way Jeanette had been dolled up like Joanie had never seen her before.

What could possibly be going on? It can't be. I must be wrong.

"Joanie."

It was a male voice, a familiar male voice.

No!

It had come from her left and, without a beat, she decided to pretend not to have heard it. She looked at the stores to her right, in the opposite direction of the voice, and picked up her pace.

"Joanie Deetz!" The male voice was louder now.

She knew who it was.

There was no avoiding it.

Joanie slowed and turned around.

It was Brodie Enoch, arm-in-arm with his wife, Jeanette, whose brown eyes were so large and whose face was so red with embarrassment, she looked as if she'd just gotten caught red-handed with another man.

Joanie was shellshocked, too, and her face felt as hot as Jeanette's looked. The only words she could muster were, "Hi there."

"What brings you down here?" Brodie said.

Jeanette smiled briefly and looked back and forth, everywhere but at Joanie. Her thick makeup looked as if she'd had it professionally done. She was beautiful.

Joanie spoke up. "I . . . had a return—for Brandon and Kristen. Wedding gift."

"Ahh," Brodie said. "Are they still on their honeymoon?" Twitch, twitch.

Jeanette continued to smile shyly on and off, and looked left and right, up and down. She was nervous as a cat. But why? Because she'd been caught wearing Joanie's dress and shoes? Could that *possibly* be? She sure was acting like it.

"They get home in a day or two," Joanie said.

Jeanette nodded agreeably but still did not look Joanie in the eyes. Then she subtly took the long, black winter coat from her arm and began putting it on. It did not even cross Brodie's mind to help her on with it.

It was then that Joanie caught a whiff of Brodie's cologne, which smelled exactly like *Dante's Dance.*

The whole thing was surreal and made Joanie feel like she was floating above the situation.

And it also made Joanie *mad.* Could they have dared enter her home? Taken their things? Joanie made up her mind right then to go on the offensive. "What about you guys? Jeanette, how are you enjoying your new house and the neighborhood?"

After an awkward pause, Brodie squeezed Jeanette's arm ever so briefly, but noticeably, as if to force her to get into the conversation like a normal person.

Jeanette's pretty cheeks flushed one deeper shade of crimson.

"It's fine. Yes. Very nice," Jeanette said, buttoning up the coat.

"We haven't met a lot of people yet," Brodie said with two quick involuntary smiles.

"Jeanette," said Joanie, "you look beautiful. I love that dress."

Brodie's dark eyes bore into Joanie's for what seemed like ten seconds, then his head swiveled toward his wife. Jeanette attempted a smile but there was no hiding the panic. She looked down at the floor and pulled her coat closed more tightly at the lapels. "Thank you," she whispered.

"Where did you find it?" Joanie said. "I have the hardest time finding unique dresses."

"You would look good in that," Brodie said, staring at Joanie brazenly.

Joanie's face flushed.

Jeanette was at a loss for words.

Brodie's head craned backward and he looked around. "I think you got it in this mall somewhere, wasn't it honey? That store that went out of business?"

Jeanette nodded shyly. "That's right. I forget the name."

"By the way, Joanie, we have a favorite restaurant in here," Brodie pointed back toward the eatery where Joanie had spotted them. "Saphire. Amazing. Expensive, but definitely worth it."

Again, Jeanette nodded in agreement and looked down at the gold high heels, which looked tight on her long, narrow feet. She wore black stockings and Joanie wondered if they were hers.

"Maybe we can all go out some time," Brodie said. "The four of us." His shoulder twitched several times. Jeanette stared at the fancy clothing store to her left and bobbed on her toes.

"Mm," Joanie said, thinking that would be a nightmare.

Brodie made a bit more small talk, mentioning several restaurants they had enjoyed up by their neighborhood, none of which Joanie and Wayne frequented.

When Brodie finally stopped talking for two seconds to take a breath, Joanie said, "Listen, I have to run. It's nice to see you both."

Jeanette's whole body twisted and she seemed to breathe a sigh of relief, finally glancing ever so briefly into Joanie's eyes.

Joanie froze.

Jeanette's eyes glistened.

Her dark eyebrows arched for a split-second.

There was a haunting depth or some sort of longing in Jeanette's eyes.

Brodie had not seen it.

But Joanie had.

12

———

It seemed odd for Roxanne to admit such a thing, but she liked having Randall around the house. She got so lonely all by herself. Without him there, her days often turned into just a blur of work, fast food, alcohol, TV, snacking, and sleepless nights. At least with Randall she had someone to interact with, to cook for, to talk to—even if he wasn't the most unselfish man alive. There was a side to Randall others didn't see. He could be caring and compassionate. He could be generous. But only when he wasn't drinking.

Over the past few days, they'd somehow managed not only to get the information they needed from old Mrs. Jensen, but one other elderly widow as well. Randall was giddy and had promised Roxanne he would be leaving soon, and that he would be giving her a substantial financial reward for her assistance.

She had a rare Saturday off and was catching up on laundry and getting all of Randall's clothes clean before he left. Dare she ask him if he might want to stay a bit longer? Oh, she knew that was a crazy thought. But, when they had been married all those years ago, they did have some good times. Randall did have that good side, and Roxanne wondered if she might be able to rekindle that version of him.

Randall came in from the cluttered garage and a cold breeze swept in with him. He shut the door with a comment about how

62

frigid it was and turned around carrying the larger of the two suit-cases he owned.

"I should have had my own business," he said proudly, hoisting the black suitcase up in the air, then setting it down and rolling it on the kitchen floor. "You see this retractable handle?" He pointed to the long arm on the suitcase.

"Yes, dear," Roxanne said.

"It was broken, okay? Wouldn't pull up, wouldn't push down; it was as if it was locked. I got in there, got to the innards of the thing, and actually super-glued a small piece of metal to the little tabby thing in there, which was broken, and, voila!" He pushed the long handle down and pulled it up, repeatedly.

"Amazing," Roxanne said. "Do you have anything else that needs to be cleaned. I'm on my last load."

"You have everything, my dear. Thank you for doing that."

Aww, there was the side of him she used to love.

"You're welcome. Where will you go now?"

"Not sure. I know a guy down in Eugene who I need to see at some point. Owes me some money—and a favor—so I may go down there. Then I was thinking about Vegas. I've had good luck there in the past—there's a lot of gullible tourists wandering that old Strip."

"Randall?" she said while folding his T-shirts.

"Yeah, baby."

"Would you ever consider settling down, staying in one place for a while?"

"Huh." He crossed his arms and made a funny face with a scrunched-up frown. "Where are you going with that?"

"I just wondered if you would ever want to stay in one place, establish a residence, stop moving around so much? You're not getting any younger."

Randall walked over to the couch where Roxanne was seated and sat down next to her. He put a hand out and stopped her from folding the clothes for a moment. He looked into her eyes.

"I wish I could, Roxy. I wish a lot of things." He looked down.

It had been a long, long time since Roxanne had seen Randall show any sentiment.

"Like what?" she said. "What do you wish?"

He looked at her and shook his head and suddenly tears filled his big, sad, fading eyes. "I wish I'd finished high school. Maybe gone to college. Found a career; an honest career."

Roxanne reached over and covered his big hands with her small hands. "It's not too late for that."

He laughed and sniffed.

"I don't mean get an education," she said. "I mean, you can still pursue an honest career."

"Look at me, Roxy." He put his hands out and looked down at himself. "I'm obese. I don't exercise. I have untreated high blood pressure and probably diabetes. Alcohol has a wicked grip on me. I'm just an ugly old man. I hate getting old."

She began to defend him, to give him hope, but he cut her off.

"Plus, I haven't made an honest dime my whole life." He stood abruptly and walked to the small fireplace and leaned on the mantel with his back to her. His shoulders lurched.

He was crying.

Roxanne froze where she was. She'd never seen this. She felt so sad for him.

"I've hurt people," he blurted. "Destroyed lives. Stolen people's life savings." He turned to face her, his face red and wet with tears. "I'm the worst of the worst, Roxy. I belong in hell for what I've done to people. Innocent people. People who lived right. Saved. Invested! They did it all right! And I—"

"Randall."

"I took it all from them. Who am I to do that?" He was yelling now. "What in the world could be worse than what I've done?"

Roxanne was in tears.

Randall crossed the room, went into the kitchen, and got a can of Pabst from the fridge. He popped the top, put his head back, and drank half the can.

Roxanne stood up and went to him. She touched his arm. "Kristen and Brandon go to church. All the Deetzes do, too. They're good people. We could go to church, Randall. I've thought about it ever since Kristen started going. She's changed. We can change. I need to, too. I drink too much. My life is a mess."

"I'm just sorry I've made you a part of . . . the scams. That's a dirty, nasty trick on my part."

She just stared at him. He was right. It had been selfish of him to ask her to commit crimes. She regretted it, too. It made her feel filthy—and sad. She was always sad, it seemed. And she was scared that if he got caught—which he very well could—she would go to prison.

"I promise you, Roxy, I would never tell anyone you helped me," he said.

She nodded. "Thank you. You better not."

He came back into the room with his beer and sat in a chair next to her.

They looked at each other, silent for a long time.

"You could get a job around here someplace," she said. "An honest job."

He huffed and sipped his beer. "No one can pay me what I bring in now; not even close."

"I'd let you stay here, rent free, if you got an honest job."

"Look at me, Roxy. No one wants to hire a washed-up old man."

"You don't know that. Even a job at Home Depot or Lowe's to start. I can cover our groceries, utilities, all that. I do it now, so it's no stretch for me."

Randall smiled and leaned back in his chair. "That's the Roxanne I remember. So kind. You deserve better than living in this little dump, burning the candle at both ends, scratching to survive." He paused for a long time. "I should have taken better care of you. I know that. I think about it often, believe it or not. And Kristen . . . she hates me. I don't blame her."

"Is it too late?" she said, looking at him with pleading eyes.

He set the beer can down on the coffee table and leaned closer to her. "You tempt me, Roxanne. You really do. But—"

Her heart raced. "Then do something about it. We can go out today—right now—and you can start turning in job applications. I'll drive. I know just where to start—"

He closed his eyes, shook his head, reached over, and took her hand.

"Roxy. I wish I could. I really do. But you deserve better than me, and—"

"I'll decide what I deserve. I wouldn't be suggesting this if I didn't want to."

He stood, crossed in front of her, and sat down next to her on the couch. He wrapped his big arms around her, and she, him.

They simply held each other.

Roxanne could hear the wall clock ticking.

It was as if she was waiting for a verdict. Waiting for his next words. Waiting to see whether her life might finally change for the better. Or would it be better? Most of the time, Randall was a crude, callous man who thought only of himself. Why was she pretending that would change?

It didn't matter. Roxanne needed something. Her life was stale as old bread. She would gamble on this. She leaned back and looked at him. He leaned back and looked at her.

"I can't stay here, Roxy."

She started to appease him, but he cut her off. "You wouldn't be safe."

That stopped her cold.

Confusion clouded her mind.

Why would she not be safe?

He could see the concern in her eyes.

"I've hurt too many people." He leaned back on the couch. His head dropped back and he stared at the ceiling. "That's why I have to keep moving. As they say, I've made my bed."

"Is it really that bad?" she said.

He continued leaning his head back and closed his eyes. "Yes. In fact, I've stayed here too long."

"Okay, just thinking out loud—what if I came with you?"

"Huh. No. That wouldn't work, baby. Believe me. For ten thousand reasons, it wouldn't work." He leaned forward, picked up the beer can, and drank.

Roxanne's heart sank.

She knew him well enough to know not to pursue it.

"In fact," he groaned as he got to his feet and stretched. "I need to hit the highway here pretty soon."

Roxanne pulled the laundry basket closer and resumed folding.

He walked toward the small, dark hallway.

He stopped and turned back toward her before going to his room.

"Thank you, Roxy."

She looked up at him. "You're welcome. And, if you ever change your mind about staying here, the door will be open."

He blinked and smiled and nodded.

Then he slapped the doorframe and disappeared down the hallway.

Roxanne cried softly as she finished folding the clothes.

13

———

Sergeant Dolby Tidwell sat with Wayne and Joanie Deetz over lunch at their kitchen table. It was a Saturday and both men were off work. Tidwell had come over to the Deetz's house as a favor, to possibly go with Wayne to pay a visit to Brodie and Jeanette Enoch's house next door, in the aftermath of the break-in a week earlier.

"So, you got home from seeing the Enochs at Portland Plaza of Shoppes—"

"And I checked for the red dress," Joanie said. "It's definitely gone."

"And you think it was the *exact* dress? *Your* dress?" Tidwell said.

"No doubt in my mind. And the shoes! They were too small for her. Those were my shoes, maybe even my stockings. It's so creepy, Dolby. I can't even get my head around it."

"Well, they certainly didn't expect to run into you all the way down in that part of town," Tidwell said.

"No way," Deetz said.

"And the thing is, Dolby, she never looks like she did that day," Joanie said. "I mean, she looked like a Hollywood celebrity. Hair. Makeup. Everything to the nines. And around here . . . well, she's so shy she runs into the house if she sees either of us. She often wears a mask."

"No makeup," Deetz added. "Big, baggy jeans or long dresses. Like Little House on the Prairie."

"Hmm." Tidwell took another bite of his chicken salad sandwich, then wiped his mouth with his napkin. "And you ran a background check?"

"Yeah. I couldn't find anything on either of them."

"It is possible they were just out for a romantic lunch," Tidwell said. "And is it possible she found the same dress and shoes as you own, Joanie. And even the cologne; he could own his own bottle of Dante's Dance, or it could be something that smells just like it. I'm trying to give them every possible out here."

"What are you saying? You think we should drop it?" Deetz said. "Just wait it out?"

Tidwell's broad shoulders bounced, and he threw his hands up. "Look, no matter how you slice it, this is a sticky wicket. These are your next-door neighbors. Brand new. And the second we go over there and imply in any way that they had something to do with your break-in, well, that will be the end of any relationship with them, I would think. And that kind of a breach will probably last as long as you live here."

Deetz looked at Joanie. He hated to see the fear and anger dancing in her eyes.

"I mean, I'm game to go over there right now," Tidwell said, "but I don't have to live here. I think it's wise for you guys to talk it all through first, think out loud, weigh the repercussions. That would give you time to get a search warrant."

"You can't just search it based on probable cause?" Joanie said.

Tidwell shook his head. "Probable cause gets you the search warrant. If we go over there right now without one, the only way we can search it, officially, is if they give us consent. Of course, we could say we want to search it and they may not insist on a warrant if they don't know the law."

"Okay, what if you go over right now, search it, and find our things—"

"One or both of them will be arrested," Tidwell said.

"And if we don't find anything, we leave with our tail between our legs, and we've made enemies of our neighbors," Deetz said.

"You sound like you don't want to confront them now," Joanie said in a frustrated tone. "I'm ninety-five percent sure they did this. We prayed about it, Wayne. That's why Dolby's here. What are we waiting for?"

Deetz nodded slowly. "I know, honey. I just don't want to do anything we'll regret."

"I mean, I could go in there with someone else, another detective or officer instead of you, Wayne, but the Enochs are still going to clearly understand that you two pointed the finger at them as suspects, that you think they broke into your house and took your things. That's a heavy insinuation."

Deetz groaned, thinking what an awkward and awful situation it was. He hated conflict.

"What it comes down to is one of two things," Tidwell said. "We go over there right now and tell them what you suspect, and hopefully search the house and make an arrest, or you forget about it for now, keep your eyes open, and get a search warrant."

"Think about it, honey, if we go over now and they don't give us consent—because they know we'd find our things—then we have to get a warrant and by then they will have gotten rid of all the evidence."

"I'm sorry, but I'm not scared of them and I'm feeling an urgency about this." Joanie pushed her chair back and began gathering up empty plates. "My vote is for you to go over there, right now. You're going to find our things, I promise you."

Tidwell's eyebrows shot up and down.

Deetz felt the weight of the world on his back. He was torn about what to do. He hated to add fuel to the fire in the conflict with the neighbors, but Joanie probably wasn't going to rest until he confronted them.

Deetz leveled his gaze with Tidwell. "Shall we?"

AFTER RINGING the doorbell at the Enoch's front door, Deetz and Tidwell stood there and commiserated about what a rough winter it had been as the wind and drizzle whipped in on them. Deetz was nervous and Tidwell did most of the talking. Deetz noticed a security camera in a corner above them. The Enoch's garage door was closed and Brodie's Wrangler was parked in the driveway.

"You think they're home?" Tidwell said.

Deetz's stomach churned. He glanced up at the camera so Tidwell would notice it. Then he whispered, "That's his Wrangler and she always parks in the garage. They're here."

Tidwell stepped over and rang the doorbell again.

They both heard movement inside and looked at each other.

"Someone's home," Tidwell said.

Footsteps approached inside and the door nudged open, but only about six inches.

Jeanette Enoch stared at them but said nothing. She wore a white mask that covered her nose and mouth. Her skin was pale and her sad eyes were sunk in as if she hadn't eaten in days. Her hair was rather a mess. Deetz couldn't tell what she was wearing because the door was only open ajar.

"Hi Jeanette," Deetz said. "This is Sergeant Dolby Tidwell. We work together at the Portland Police Bureau. Do you mind if we step inside for a minute?"

Her dark eyes flicked to Tidwell and back to Deetz. "Brodie's on a business call right now." She spoke softly and didn't budge.

"That's okay," Deetz said. "We're here to see both of you. Can we come in?"

She looked back into the house for a good ten seconds, then turned back to face them. She pulled the mask down below her chin.

"This really isn't the best time." Her cheeks had flushed. "Can you come back later?"

Deetz did not want to give them time to hide evidence.

"Mrs. Enoch," Tidwell said in his deep, imposing voice, "we need to come in now." He stepped closer to the door. "It won't take long. Promise."

Deetz felt the tension ratchet up.

Without a word, Jeanette stepped back as Tidwell gently pushed the door open and led the way inside. Deetz, who had never been in the house, followed the big sergeant.

The house was dark, especially for the middle of day.

It smelled like cats.

Jeanette wore an oversized brown sweater over a white turtle-neck, a long denim dress, and simple black slip-on shoes with no heels.

"What is it you need?" said Jeanette, turning around to scan the downstairs. "If it's about the break-in at your house, Brodie is the one who saw the van."

Deetz stammered. "In a way it is about the break-in. This is rather awkward. I know you and Brodie ran into Joanie at Portland Plaza recently."

Jeanette's small mouth sealed shut. Her nostrils flared. She was visibly anxious and embarrassed.

"Joanie said you were wearing a dress and shoes that . . . that were missing from our house after the break-in."

Jeanette's mouth opened slightly and she froze. She seemed unable to look at either man. She stared at the space between them.

Deetz and Tidwell shot raised eyebrows at each other.

After several more seconds, Jeanette's sunken eyes moved upward and locked on Tidwell.

Her face was red.

A tear leaked out her right eye.

Suddenly, Deetz felt as if she was in trouble—dark, frightful trouble.

"Jeanette," Deetz leaned close to her and spoke softly, "is something going on here, with Brodie? Do you need our help?"

Deetz heard movement upstairs. So did Tidwell.

"Tell us, Jeanette," Tidwell said. "We can help you."

Her left hand reached out and touched Tidwell's arm. Her right hand covered her mouth.

She looked as if she was about to spill her guts.

A loud noise came from upstairs.

"Jeanette?" Brodie yelled loudly. "What's going on?" His voice came closer.

Deetz heard him thumping down the stairs.

"Jeanette?" Brodie called.

How could he know the exact time to come out?

Deetz looked at Tidwell with a suspicious scowl.

Could he have the downstairs bugged—with a speaker up in his office? Or even cameras?

Brodie rounded the corner leading into the foyer. "Ah, who do we have here?" His voice was loud and fraught with nervous anxiety that he was trying to cover up.

He approached wearing his usual, rugged hiker attire, looking at Deetz and Tidwell, then at Jeanette.

He embraced his wife. "What's wrong, baby?"

He twitched several times and squinted at Tidwell, then Deetz.

"What could *possibly* be going on here?" he demanded.

14

———

ROXANNE HUMMED LIGHTHEARTEDLY as she drove back home following her secret trip to Kristen and Brandon's new apartment. She'd gotten word from Kristen that the newlyweds would be arriving home from Hawaii that evening, as scheduled, so she'd decided to fill their fridge with goodies so they wouldn't have to run out to the store right after the long trip home. She'd gotten lunchmeat, eggs, bread, fresh fruit and veggies, and even a bottle of sparkling cider. She'd also baked them a batch of Christmas cookies.

She turned onto her street, splashing through puddles and wishing they would get a break in the weather. They'd had rain and frigid temps for the past week. She hoped Brandon wouldn't mind that Kristen had given her the code to their new place. Of course, she only planned to use it on occasions such as this. Oh, and of course, when the baby came—she might be needed to pop in quickly now and then.

Roxanne was feeling satisfied and happy, knowing the groceries would bless the tired newlyweds. She was also feeling a bit giddy, wondering if they would have a boy or a girl, and what they might name it. Perhaps, if it was a girl, they would consider Roxanne as a middle name!

Roxanne's little house came into view through the rain-streaked car windows, and she noticed a black sedan parked in the driveway at rather an odd angle.

She got a check in her spirit and slowed way down as she drove along the front of the property toward the driveway. She didn't know anyone with a car like that and wondered if it was someone Randall knew.

Instead of pulling in, Roxanne continued driving slowly past the house. She dialed Randall's cell phone and drove back through the neighborhood, thinking she would make a circle and come back.

As she drove along, the call went to his voice mail.

She hung up and picked up the pace as she circled around the familiar streets back to the front edge of her property.

She could feel her heart tapping in the upper part of her chest as she pulled into the grass, stopped her car, and watched the strange car and the house.

Deetz and Tidwell looked at each other in the dark foyer of the Enoch house after Brodie Enoch had practically run down the stairs and made the fiery comment, "What could *possibly* be going on here?"

Jeanette backed up several feet and stood there with her slender white fingers locked together like a vice in front of her face.

"Brodie, this is my sergeant, Dolby Tidwell," Deetz said.

Tidwell extended his hand, but Brodie ignored it and stuck his hands on his waist and tapped his foot.

"As I was telling Jeanette," Deetz said, "Joanie mentioned running into you two at the Portland Plaza of Shoppes recently."

Brodie's whole head twitched several times, but he just stood there steaming.

"Joanie said Jeanette had on a dress and shoes that looked exactly like hers—some of the items that were stolen during our break-in."

Brodie's head dropped for several seconds, then lifted. "Okay, what is this, Wayne?" Brodie waved a hand. "What are you imply-ing?" His voice and mannerism became quick and choppy. "That

Jeanette broke into your house—with a crowbar—and stole your wife's things? Are you for real right now?"

"He actually wasn't implying it was your wife, Mr. Enoch," said Tidwell in a low, serious tone. "Now, because Mrs. Deetz saw the dress and shoes, we have probable cause to search the house. Are you good with that?"

Deetz held his breath, hoping Brodie wouldn't know enough to hold out for a search warrant.

Brodie's jaw clamped like a vice and he blinked involuntarily.

"So . . . this is how we welcome new neighbors!" Brodie swung around dramatically with an outstretched arm. "Search all you want. You're not going to find anything. This is just great, Wayne. After the way we've reached out to you?"

Deetz began to follow Tidwell around the corner toward the stairs anxious to get out of Brodie's sight.

"Did you forget I'm the one who reported the break-in?" Brodie yelled. "I'll tell you this, I better not find one *breadcrumb* out of place, or I'll sue you and your whole department!"

As they climbed the steps, Deetz heard Brodie snap at Jeanette, *"Get. Over. Here."*

Tidwell found the master bedroom and flicked on an overhead light, and Deetz followed him in. Without a word, they both pulled drawers open, one after another. Deetz found all the clothes in the drawers to be folded perfectly—all neat and tidy.

Deetz checked under the bed and saw nothing except the silhouette of a cat, which initially spooked him. He joined Tidwell in the closet where the two men searched high and low.

"I've never seen anything so . . . organized," Tidwell said.

"Yeah. I don't see the red dress or the shoes—or any of Joanie's things."

"Or cologne of any kind. Let's keep looking."

They split up and covered the other rooms upstairs, turning on lights as they went.

Deetz got to one room that featured three large computer screens, several keyboards, a big cushy set of headphones, a professional looking microphone, and a swivel chair. He figured it was Brodie's office, because he worked remotely most of the time. There was a crooked poster of a downhill snow skier on one wall and a rock climber on another, like things you'd see in the bedroom of a high school or college student. There were two enormous cat scratching post towers in two corners of the room, along with a litter box. The smell of cats was almost overwhelming.

If Brodie and Jeanette did have anything to do with the break-in at Deetz's house, he was convinced the stolen items were in some secret hiding place, if in the house at all.

In the hallway ceiling, Deetz spotted pull-down steps to the attic, but there was no way to reach them. Tidwell met Deetz in the hallway holding a two-foot wood rod with a hook on the end. "Great minds," Deetz said.

They eyed each other, nodded, and Tidwell used the tool to reach up and pull the attic stepladder down. Deetz climbed up the steps and peered around in the attic using the light from his phone. It was as tidy as the clothes in their drawers and closets. The floor was blanketed with pink insulation and there was nothing up there except several filters for the furnace.

By the time Deetz got back down and folded the attic ladder up into the ceiling, Tidwell had begun searching the downstairs. Deetz joined him.

"Come on, Jeanette," Brodie barked, crossing to the steps. "Let's stay out of their way."

Brodie waited for timid Jeanette to start up the stairs and he followed.

Deetz did not like the way he bossed her around. He felt sorry for her. And he was concerned for her wellbeing.

As they silently searched cupboards, cabinets, and drawers, Deetz came to the sober realization that they weren't going to find anything. He felt Tidwell probably thought the same.

If the red dress and gold shoes were Jeanette's, why weren't they in the master closet?

"Should we bring up the dress and shoes?" Deetz whispered to Tidwell.

Tidwell frowned and tilted his head. "I'd like to hear his excuse."

"I'll get them." Deetz went to the bottom of the staircase, called up, and told the Enochs they were finished with the search.

Deetz heard whispering in the hallway upstairs and then Brodie bounced down the steps, without Jeanette.

"So, what did we find, gentlemen?" Brodie said in a sarcastic tone. "Am I under arrest?"

"Is Jeanette coming?" Tidwell said.

"Is she needed?" Brodie threw up his hands. "Haven't you embarrassed us enough for one day?"

Tidwell cut in. "Where's the red dress and shoes she had on at Portland Plaza when you saw Joanie?"

Brodie froze for an instant with his mouth hanging open and blinked repeatedly. "I haven't the foggiest what you're talking about."

Tidwell took several giant steps to the staircase and called up, "Mrs. Enoch, can you please come down here?"

Brodie took several steps toward the stairs and watched his shy wife come down, quiet as a mouse. She had the germ mask covering her nose and mouth again. Brodie glared at her the whole way. She came and stood next to her husband.

"Where is the red dress and shoes you had on when you saw Joanie Deetz at the Portland Plaza of Shoppes?" Tidwell said, point blank.

Jeanette's bony white fingers were clasped together in front of her, at her waist. Her thin shoulders swayed back and forth. She looked at the floor, at her husband, then at the ceiling, and around the room. "I don't own a red dress. And the shoes . . . I never . . ." She shook her head.

"Red's never been her color," Brodie added.

"You're saying Joanie is lying," Deetz said.

Jeanette was about to say something when Brodie interrupted. "We saw Joanie that day, but Jeanette wasn't wearing a red dress, she doesn't even own one. Or gold shoes."

"We never even described the shoes," Deetz snapped. "How do you even—"

"You don't have to!" Brodie yelled and shook his fists. "We didn't take your things! Now are you done here?"

Jeanette folded her thin arms, fidgeted with the mask, and repeatedly swayed and shifted on her feet. It was painful just watching the fretfulness pent up within her. Deetz feared for what was going on in that house, feared the mental and physical torment she may be going through.

15

Roxanne shut off her car because the exhaust fumes were visible in the cold air and she didn't want to risk being spotted. As the minutes ticked by, she became more and more anxious about what was happening inside her house with Randall and whomever had arrived in the black car. She contemplated calling Wayne Deetz to come over, but she wasn't even sure Randall was in trouble. Knowing him, the owner of the car could be a long-lost pal of some sort. She listened intently with her car windows down a crack, but she could hear nothing.

Several minutes later the front door of her little house burst open and a huge man wearing a dark suit and overcoat came rambling out.

Roxanne slid down in her seat, her heart thumping.

With gloved hands, the bald man yanked a black ski hat from his coat pocket and pulled it onto his wide head, spit, then buttoned up the coat as he headed for the car. Seconds later, another man followed. This one was average size, bundled up in a green parka, hat, and gloves. He stopped briefly to light a cigarette, then hurried on, and repeatedly glanced back at the house as he headed for the passenger side of the sedan.

Roxanne ducked lower and waited as the car straightened by pulling forward, then backed out of the driveway at a good clip.

Once it was out of sight, she started her car and pulled it in.

She couldn't think of much else besides making sure Randall was okay.

She hurried inside and called his name but heard no response.

Not good. This is not good.

She called again as she frantically scurried from the kitchen into the family room with her coat still on.

After searching every room, she got to the small guest bathroom, stuck her head in and screamed when she saw him lying in the bathtub. Splotches of blood dotted his gray sweatpants and sweatshirt. His face was badly beaten and bloody; one eye was swollen shut.

He groaned when she got to him.

Roxanne shook terribly from the shock of the sight. She managed to get her phone out of her coat pocket, but she dropped it because her hands were trembling so badly. She scrambled for the phone.

"Don't, Roxy. Don't call," Randall murmured.

She argued, but with all the strength in him he urged her not to call an ambulance or police.

He was like a beached whale.

"How can I help you?" she squirmed. "What can I do?"

"Get some towels," he said softly. "Soak them in water."

She quickly did as he said and by the time she got to him he had worked his way into a sitting position. Blood was smeared everywhere.

He put one of the wet towels over his head and dabbed the blood from his battered face.

"What happened?" She was afraid to touch him. "Who did this, Randall?"

He grunted and put the towel around his neck. He pushed the other towel up under his sweatshirt to stop some of the bleeding.

"Help me up, will you?" he said.

She knew not to argue. Hesitantly, she took his left arm and did what she could, but he was a huge man.

As he was about to stand, he slipped on the blood in the tub and cursed, but somehow kept his balance.

The sudden movement and scare made Roxanne yelp.

With much effort and pain, Randall worked his way into a full standing position. He stood there gingerly with one bloody hand against the aqua colored tile wall and one on Roxanne's shoulder, getting his bearings.

"Help me out, please."

Roxanne steadied him as he climbed out of the tub.

"Throw an old blanket on your bed," he said. "Get me some peroxide and triple antibiotic ointment or Vaseline—gauze and bandages; butterfly bandages if you have any. More towels, too. And a mirror. I'll sit there to bandage up. I don't want to make a mess of your house. I'm sorry about this, Roxy. I should have left yesterday."

Roxanne ran into her bathroom nearly tripping on a rug in the hallway. That was all they needed. She got to the linen closet and gathered up everything he'd requested. She spread the old blanket onto her bed just as he was getting there. He sat down on the edge of the bed with a huff.

"Clean up that blood, before it stains your floors." He nodded toward the path he'd taken from the bathroom.

"Oh, good grief, I'm not worried about that."

"Trust me, it'll stain if you don't get it up. Don't worry about me. This'll take me a while."

"Oh, for Pete's sake." She scurried off, got a mop and bucket of hot water and did the best she could with the blood droplets that trailed their way from the guest bathroom to her bed. She also washed down the bathtub and cleaned it up as best she could, working up a sweat.

By the time she got back to Randall, he had undressed down to his white underwear and socks. His chest and back and legs were badly bruised, and he was bandaging and taping several of the more severe wounds.

"What did they use, a bat? Did they kick you?" She was sickened at the sight of the bludgeoning he'd taken.

A tear slipped down his rough face.

Roxanne noticed he was shivering so she dashed out and turned the heat up. She also fetched another blanket. She heard the heat kick on as she got back to him.

"I turned the heat up," she said, out of breath. "Maybe you can wrap yourself up in this for a while." She held the blanket up.

He nodded and welcomed the blanket as she draped it around his large shoulders.

Randall was overweight, but he was also just a solid man. Big and strong.

"You want to go to the recliner?" Roxanne said.

He shook his head. "If you can prop some pillows up, I think I'll just sit here for a while."

Without a word she went to work, making the bed as comfortable as possible.

He seemed different.

Humbled? Ashamed? Defeated?

"I'm sorry about all this, Roxanne."

She helped him get situated leaning his back against the pillows at the headboard of the bed.

"What can I get you?" she said.

"Whiskey."

She stood and headed out of the room.

"No ice, please," he called.

ROXANNE HANDED the bourbon glass to Randall, who was still shivering even though he was wrapped in the large blanket. He was sitting up now, resting his back and head against several large pillows.

He thanked her and took a sip. "Ahh."

She sat close to him on the edge of the bed and produced a small bag of ice. "You need to put this on that eye."

He closed his eyes and leaned his head back against the headboard, holding the glass in front of him. A butterfly bandage held a cut together high on his cheek beneath the good eye, and another did the same at the top of his forehead.

"Who were they?" she said, forcing the bag of ice into one hand.

He took the ice bag and gently held it against the swollen eye.

He was tough. Didn't complain.

"They were hired by someone I conned," he said.

"Who? Who hired them?"

He leaned his head forward, took a sip of whiskey, and leaned back.

He chuckled. "Believe it or not, it's an old widow in Utah." He shook his head in disbelief. "She hired a private investigator. He tracked me down. Then she hired these goons."

"To get the money back that you swindled from her?"

He nodded. "That's never happened."

"The chickens always come home to roost, Randall."

He smirked. "I guess so."

"So, what now?"

"I have a week. Christmas day."

"To get them how much money?"

He handed her the ice bag and swigged the booze.

"You don't want to know," he said.

Roxanne squirmed. All kinds of thoughts ran through her head.

"Can you get it? Do you have it? What about the funds we got the other day?"

He chuckled. "That was chump change compared to this. No, I don't have it and no I can't get it by then."

"So, what?" Roxanne was panicked and getting angry. "Am I in danger Randall?"

Her heart, her home, her future just hung there in the balance, in the hands of this . . . this man, this con artist! She hated him and loved him at the same time.

Randall sat there in silence with a furrowed brow, staring at the glass in his hands.

She could wring his neck!

"Say something!" she yelled.

He shook his head. "I'm thinking. I've got to come up with a plan."

"Oh, you and your plans and schemes. It's nothing but smoke and mirrors. You need to get out of here, Randall."

"It's not that easy, Roxanne. They'll be back. They said if I leave . . ."

"What?" Roxanne said. "They'll do something to me?"

"I can't leave you here alone," he said. "In fact, we probably need to find someplace for you to go."

16

———

IT WAS a cozy Sunday afternoon in the den at the Deetz residence, where the Christmas tree was lit, and Wayne had a nice fire blazing and crackling in the fireplace. He and Joanie and Leena had gone to church on that wet, cold morning, and had changed into sweatpants, hoodies, and slippers for the afternoon. J.P. and Tammy were there cuddled up on the couch, as were the newlyweds, Brandon and Kristen, who had arrived home from Hawaii the night before.

Everyone lounged around talking and laughing as they munched bowls of Joanie's popular, specially seasoned popcorn. Brandon and Kristen seemed relaxed and happy as they projected photos from their phones onto the TV screen above the fireplace and described some of their favorite moments from the trip.

For Deetz, it was rather a relief when he and Joanie finally got around to sharing with the family their suspicions about the Enochs, and the fact that Joanie had run into Brodie and Jeanette at Portland Plaza, and that Deetz and Tidwell had actually confronted them and searched their house.

Of course, this juicy new twist in their parents' lives caused all the kids to go ballistic.

"So, let me get this straight," Brandon said. "Mom saw Mrs. Enoch wearing what she *thinks* was her dress and shoes—"

"I don't 'think,' I know," Joanie said.

85

"But aren't these things you could get anywhere, like the Mercantile or Nordstrom?" Brandon said.

"That may be so," Joanie said, "but my exact dress and shoes were taken in the robbery and then there they were, on someone who *never* dresses up."

"Mom, I love you, but it just seems like a stretch," Brandon said. "Even if you do think they're guilty—to send Dad and Tidwell over there, accusing them and searching the house! I mean, oh my gosh."

"Not the best way to make new friends," J.P. joked.

"Why didn't Dad find the dress and shoes in the search then?" Joanie said. "They lied when they said she wasn't wearing those things that day. It was a flat out lie. They got rid of them after seeing me. Who do you believe, the neighbors you don't know or your mom?"

Deetz chimed in. "We think they ditched the dress and shoes because, if we did find them and test them, they would have Mom's DNA on them."

Silence fell over the room as the kids realized how serious their parents were about the potential guilt of their next-door neighbors.

For a while, the only sound came from the spitting fire.

"Dad said there was a weird vibe in the house when he and Dolby were there," Joanie said.

"Something wasn't right—between them," Deetz said. "She's always been extremely shy and tentative anyway. When we were going upstairs, I heard him snap at her. And just the way he treated her, even in front of us, was kind of that dominant, authoritative thing. She acts like a frightened animal."

"That doesn't sound good," said Tammy, the social worker and justice seeker. "I'm glad you did the search."

Brandon suddenly shot to his feet.

"Oh my gosh, you scared me," Kristen said.

"Sorry, babe." He touched her knee. "I'm going to go get that gift they got us. Maybe it'll give us some more clues!" He dashed out of the room and everyone chuckled.

Joanie asked Kristen about their flights. Kristen answered them and told how her mom had left them the champagne and goodies.

"That was so thoughtful," Joanie said.

"It was really nice," Kristen said. "She's got a good heart."

Leena spoke up. "I'm assuming everyone got my Christmas wish list. We're only a week away from the big day."

The room broke out in laughter again.

"I'm serious," Leena said. "I think I texted everyone."

"Yeah, we all got your list like a month or two ago," J.P. said.

"You've sent it several times," Deetz said.

"Let me just tell you, you're not getting everything on that list, young lady," Joanie said. "Your dad and I are simplifying this year."

"Oh, brother, here we go," Leena moaned.

"No, I mean it," Joanie said. "We are doing one or two gifts for each person and maybe some cash."

Brandon came back into the room carrying a white box about the size of a soccer ball, from the Enochs.

"This thing is heavy." He set it on the couch next to Kristen. "You do the honors, babe."

"If you say so." She turned and untied the gold bow. Then she began lifting the top of the box and told Brandon to hold the bottom while she did so. He gripped it firmly while Kristen finally got the top off, which she held above her head.

"Looks like a candle," she said. "A *big* candle. Yum, it smells good."

"Here, I'll get it." Brandon reached into the box with both hands and lifted out a large, square candle made of dark blue glass. "Ahh, not bad. It's got four wicks. I think it's one of those that makes sounds like a campfire."

As Kristen looked at the other side of the candle, her mouth dropped open. She gasped and a hand shot to her mouth. Her eyes were the size of saucers.

After seeing her reaction, Brandon turned the candle to see the side she was looking at.

His jaw dropped and his dark eyebrows arched, then his eyes went to each person in the room.

Deetz could see the embarrassment on his son's crimson face.

Kristen appeared in shock. "That's not true!" she said.

With a look of utter disbelief on his face, Brandon slowly held up the candle and turned it so the others could see the bold, black typography printed on a white label: *NO LONGER LIVING IN SIN.*

"What on earth." Deetz vaulted to the edge of his seat.

Joanie was on her feet, examining the candle, checking the empty box.

"Now that is completely unhinged," J.P. said.

"I can't believe that," Tammy said. "It has to be a mistake. Did it come right from a store? Maybe they sent the wrong thing."

"We *didn't* live together." Kristen had tears in her eyes. "Who are these people?"

"Did someone tell them Kris is pregnant?" Brandon said.

"Absolutely not," Deetz said. "They don't know anything about us."

"I don't get it," Leena said, examining the candle.

"It's *implying* that Brandon and Kristen were living together before they got married, Leena," said Joanie. "Which they were *not* doing—"

"Oh, and so now that they're married it's saying they're no longer living in sin," Leena said. "I get it. Seems a little personal."

Wayne and Joanie had done their best to clearly explain Brandon's and Kristen's situation to Leena—how a one-time encounter had led to her pregnancy. How they had gotten married to do the right thing.

"I'm going over there," Brandon said.

"Oh no you're not." Deetz shot to his feet. "Just cool down, buddy."

"I think they ordered a different candle and somehow that got put in the box," said Tammy, who was always looking for the good in others.

Joanie shook her head. "No. This is how he rolls."

"Now I believe you," Brandon said.

"Talk about awkward," J.P. said. "I mean, how do you respond to that? *Thank you?*"

"For now, let's not say anything," Deetz said. "I feel like we need to wait it out. Time is going to expose this guy."

"I'm still in shock," Kristen said, shaking her head.

Brandon sat down beside her and took her hand.

"I'm not promising I won't say anything to them if I see them," Joanie said.

Deetz closed his eyes and didn't respond.

Because he felt the exact same way.

17

―――――

Everything about Investigator Howard Googan drove Deetz nuts. No wonder the man had gotten a divorce. He was chronically late. His aftershave was pungent. His manners were non-existent. And he wore the same clothes repeatedly, including ties with spots on them.

Currently, he was in his cubicle working at his laptop, munching on some kind of ding-dong treat from the vending machines, and sucking on a sixty-four-ounce grape slurpy he picked up at some convenience store where he got seventy-nine cent refills.

Deetz approached, wishing he wasn't responsible for the guy and counting the days until he was officially retired.

"Hey, Googan, what's the latest on the missing person I sent you?"

With a grunt, Googan swirled around in his chair and remained seated. "Hey, Deetz." His green tie was loosened, and his white dress shirt collar was unbuttoned and stained yellow. "What do you already know?"

Deetz shook his head. "Almost nothing. Woman in her thirties, possible prostitute?"

Googan motioned toward the generic spare chair in his cubicle. "You want to sit?"

Deetz did so.

"Did you know Portland has more strip clubs per capita than any other city in the U.S.?" Googan said.

"I did not."

"That's one strip club for every eleven thousand residents. That outranks Vegas, Miami, and New Orleans."

"And the point of all this is?" Deetz said.

"Just context. The missing woman is a stripper. Goes by the stage name of Dawn Delight. Her best friend reported her missing when she didn't show up for a lunch date and wasn't answering her phone." Googan swiveled left and right. "Thirty-one years young. Last seen leaving one of the clubs she dances at. It was about one-forty a.m. She'd called an Uber, but the driver says he never saw her; thinks he missed her by seconds."

"Cameras? Leads?"

"No cameras," Googan said. "Her best friend said Miss Delight has been working on getting her bachelor's degree online during days, taking like eighteen credits a semester. Hard worker. She apparently had a decent job but got laid off and hit hard times. The dancing and tips pay the bills while she goes to school. Real name's Regina Hart."

Deetz was impressed with Googan's work. Up to that moment, he'd not been positive he was going to turn over the entire missing person investigation to Googan, but now he was.

"Where does she live? Does she have family here?" Deetz said.

"She has a one-bedroom apartment in Dorsey, which, from what I understand, is a pretty nice area. Mom died from an overdose when Regina was a teenager. Dad is estranged from what I can gather."

"Any chance she just left on her own?"

"Nah." Googan shook his head. "She was abducted. Another dancer from that club, actually a male, told me Dawn has a special admirer who comes in frequently when she dances. I'm trying to learn more and track him down. May go one night and talk to some of the regulars."

"Sounds like you're on it. Good work, Googan."

"Not my first rodeo."

Urgh. Pay the guy a compliment and he returns it by patting his own back.

"Can I run with it?" Googan said.

"By all means." Deetz turned and walked away. "Keep me up to speed on any new developments."

"Yes, sir," Googan answered, sarcastically.

JOANIE WAS MAKING a late lunch of tomato soup and grilled cheese sandwiches in the kitchen for Leena and herself. Leena had just gotten home from finishing her Christmas shopping at the mall.

"Do not come in here, Mother," Leena called from the dining room where she'd set up her 'Christmas wrapping station' at the dining room table. "Did you hear me?"

Joanie smiled. "I heard you. I am not coming in there. I'm busy."

"You need to tell me if you're coming in."

"Don't worry," Joanie said. "By the way, lunch is almost ready."

"Give me five minutes," Leena called. "I need to finish this one thing I'm wrapping—before a nosy someone sees it."

Joanie snickered. Leena was such a character. Joanie set napkins and soup spoons out at the kitchen table, followed by two glasses of ice water. She still had holds to pick up at the library, and she hoped to stop by her favorite consignment shop that afternoon.

The whole saga with the Enochs was eating at her. Each time she thought about the break-in, the things that were taken, seeing the couple at the Portland Plaza, and them lying about what Jeanette was wearing, and that hideous candle they gave Brandon and Kristen—it made her sick to her stomach.

She got her phone out and turned it on to the two screenshots she'd taken early that morning. She re-read them, saying each like a prayer:

Away from me, all you who do evil,
  for the Lord has heard my weeping.
The Lord has heard my cry for mercy;
  the Lord accepts my prayer.
All my enemies will be overwhelmed
with shame and anguish;
  they will turn back and suddenly be put to shame.
— Psalm 6: 8-10

Whoever is pregnant with evil conceives trouble
and gives birth to disillusionment.
The trouble they cause recoils on them;
their violence comes down on their own heads.
— Psalm 7: 14, 16

"Mom," Leena called. "There goes Mr. Enoch."

Joanie's heart lurched in her chest.

"He's got someone in the car who isn't Mrs. Enoch," Leena said.

Joanie hurried into the dining room and went right to the window where Leena was looking out.

"You didn't announce you were coming in but it's okay because I covered up what I'm wrapping," Leena said.

Joanie only caught a glimpse of Brodie's Jeep Wrangler as it pulled into his driveway. Her view was restricted from the house.

"What did you see?" Joanie said.

"The passenger wasn't Mrs. Enoch," Leena said. "I don't know who it was."

"A woman?"

"Yep. Or a man with long hair."

Joanie checked her watch. The mail usually came about now so it wouldn't look suspicious if she went out and checked the mailbox.

"Stay here," Joanie said. "I'm going to the mailbox to see if I can see anything."

"Mom, you are really obsessing on this thing."

Joanie hurried in and turned off the burners. She checked herself in the hall mirror on the way to the front door, took a deep breath, and went out. It was cold but not raining. She walked briskly down the sidewalk with her arms crossed, to the driveway, and toward the mailbox.

Brodie's Wrangler was parked where it always was, in front of the garage.

And he was in it.

She also made out the shape of another passenger, still in the car.

The Wrangler's exhaust steamed in the cold air.

Brodie suddenly turned and caught Joanie's gaze; they were eye-to-eye for a split-second.

Joanie looked away, straight out toward the street, her heart thumping. He had lifted a hand to wave, but she kept walking as if she was simply heading to check the mail. She got to the street and turned to open the mailbox and bent down as if looking in. As she did, she glanced back at the Wrangler. Brodie remained inside with the passenger, whom Joanie could not make out.

She couldn't stand there all day staring at the empty mailbox, so she closed it and began walking slowly back down the driveway toward the house.

Brodie did not budge from the Wrangler, nor did his passenger.

Once she got back to the house, she wouldn't be able to see them anymore.

Who is that and where's Jeanette?

She thought about just marching right up to the Wrangler and saying something about that idiotic wedding gift, that way she could see the mystery passenger.

No. Wayne wouldn't go for that at all.

She had to play it cool, wait it out.

Plus, the thought of getting within reach of Brodie Enoch now terrorized her. He gave her the vibe of an abuser, a control freak, a narcissist. He was dangerous.

Her phone buzzed in her back pocket. She got it out as she walked back to the house. It was Brandon, which was odd for the middle of the day.

"Hello, Son." She took one last glance at the Wrangler before it went out of view. Brodie's back was now to the window.

"Hey, Mom," Brandon said. "How are you?"

"Fine. How about you?" She went back into the house and headed for the kitchen to finish making lunch.

"You have a minute?" he said.

That made her worry.

"Of course, what's up?"

"So . . . Roxanne wants to come stay with us for a while."

"What?" Alarms blared in Joanie's mind. "Why?"

"Randall is still at her place and, apparently, he may be in some trouble. Big surprise."

Joanie stood there frozen, shaking her head.

"Just as a precaution," Brandon continued, "she wanted to stay with us for like a week or so."

"You're newlyweds! What's she thinking?"

"That's why I called. I don't know what to do. Should we let her come?"

"What does Kristen say?"

"Neither of us are crazy about it."

"She should get an Airbnb or a hotel for a week," Joanie said.

"That's what I said but Kris talked to her and she says she can't afford it."

"Oh, hogwash. You know what, Bran, let me talk to your dad. We'll have her stay here—"

Really, in the big scope of things, it was nothing.

"No way, Mom, that's not why I called you. I just wanted to pick your brain, get your input."

"This is a small matter, Son. Let me talk to Dad and I'll call you back."

"He's not going to like it."

"We have a big house with a lot of rooms. She can stay in your old room."

"Oh, Dad's going to *love* that."

18

INVESTIGATOR WAYNE DEETZ felt a bit overwhelmed as he sat at his glowing laptop in a conference room on an upper floor at the Portland Police Bureau. He picked that spot often because he could look out the large picture window while he worked. Outside it had already gotten dark on Monday afternoon, and all he could see were the city lights through drizzling rain. He also spotted the Christmas tree atop the Peck-Howard Building, lit up in red, green, and white lights. Temps were due to dip into the low thirties that night and Christmas was only five days away.

The main thing on his mind was the call he'd received several hours earlier from Joanie, asking if Kristen's mom, Roxanne, could stay at their house for a week. Deetz's knee-jerk reaction had been an absolute no. However, as usual, Joanie had proven to be the levelheaded and generous one, insisting they would be doing everyone a favor by opening their home to Roxanne. Deetz certainly didn't want her staying with Brandon and Kristen who were just starting their new life together.

Deetz had finally agreed to host Roxanne, with one stipulation —he wanted to know why the woman had to leave her home, and what kind of trouble Randall was in. For Roxanne's sake, Randall had agreed to meet Deetz at bureau headquarters, where he was due to arrive in about thirty minutes. It rather surprised Deetz that the man would dare to set foot anywhere near a police precinct, which told Deetz that he must genuinely care about Roxanne's well-being.

Joanie had also mentioned seeing Brodie Enoch arrive home with a strange woman in his car, which hadn't fazed Deetz much. It could have been anyone—one of their sisters, a friend, a cleaning lady, anyone. Joanie never had gotten a good look at the woman. But it did bother Deetz that Joanie was on pins and needles in their own home, and he couldn't blame her. Something weird was going on next door. He couldn't get Jeanette Enoch off his mind and silently prayed for her protection.

Deetz opened Facebook and searched for Brodie Enoch. It didn't take long to find his neighbor's page and, oh man, was this guy full of himself. The huge, horizontal cover photo was an extreme closeup of Brodie's face. *Who does that?* His reading glasses sat low on his nose, and he was giving kind of a hard-guy smirk. Deetz supposed he was a rugged, fairly good-looking man. The actual small, round profile picture—where most people placed their facial shot—was a picture of him hanging on the side of a rock face, wearing sunglasses and camo-colored army-type gear.

Brodie hadn't filled in any of the bio information and his last posting had been a year earlier, so he wasn't visibly active on the page. Most of the twenty or so photos were of himself, clearly portraying a macho image, as he hiked, biked, fished, ran, rollerbladed, and kayaked. There were no other people in any of the photos, except one, and it included his wife, Jeanette, and a teenage boy and girl whom Deetz presumed were their children. Based on how old Brodie looked now, the picture had probably been taken ten to fifteen years ago. Deetz had seen that same photograph framed in their home when he and Tidwell had combed it.

Deetz searched Brodie's "friends," but could not find their two children, who were adults by now. So, Deetz figured, they could be on Facebook and just not be friends with their dad, or they may not be on Facebook at all. Brodie had perhaps fifty friends listed, many of whom were women, which was of interest.

Continuing his search, Deetz noticed that Jeanette Enoch did not have a Facebook page, at least not under her married name. *He probably didn't let her.* That was the thing about social media platforms—anyone could have an account under any fictitious name. Lurkers and scammers were everywhere.

Eventually, Deetz found a Facebook page for the son, Blake Enoch, whom he recognized from the Enoch family photo. He looked to be in his late twenties or so. In searching Blake's "friends" Deetz found the sister, who was listed under Shelly Enoch Danielson. Both adult children appeared to be married, but neither looked as if they had children.

Deetz switched over to LEDS, Oregon's police database, and searched for the daughter first. Shelly Enoch Danielson resided in Oceanside, California, was married to Steven Danielson, and was a prosecuting attorney specializing in domestic violence cases.

Next, Deetz searched for the son, Blake Enoch. Interestingly, he lived about as far away from Portland as one could, in Merritt Island, Florida, which Deetz knew was close to the Kennedy Space Center on Florida's east coast. He was married to Catherine Enoch, who worked at a private Christian school. Blake was employed by the Billings Ball Bearing Company in Melbourne, Florida.

Deetz went down the page and stopped like a deer in headlights.

He scanned the next several lines.

Catherine Enoch had called the police to the Enoch home on three separate occasions between 2016 and 2017—accusing husband Blake of threats, verbal and physical abuse, and stalking. An arrest had never been made.

Deetz was more than curious now. He checked his watch. Randall was due in fifteen minutes. He went into Google and searched, 'Blake Enoch, Catherine Enoch, domestic violence.'

What he found next moved Deetz up to the edge of his chair.

It was a magazine article in *Christianity Now*, a nationally recognized periodical. Deetz clicked the link and it opened to the main feature story in an issue dated summer 2023. There was a color photograph of a couple, smiling, sitting hand-in-hand on a couch. The cutline read, *How Blake and Catherine Enoch survived domestic violence. This is their story.*

MY CRY IN THE NIGHT
By Catherine Enoch

I'd seen only small and brief, but rather alarming flashes of my husband's domineering, violent, abusive behavior when we were dating. But this was the man I loved, the man I was going to marry. Surely, those little outbursts would go away, or I could put up with them as I had during the year and a half we had dated. It was nothing to mention to anyone or to cause me to doubt that he was the one.

Oh, how wrong I turned out to be.

To others, Blake appeared to be a handsome, attentive, generous, and protective partner. Indeed, he was those things—most of the time. But when those dark, controlling moments arose, Blake turned into a monster who humiliated me, manipulated me, terrorized me, isolated me, and abused me.

Deetz stopped reading and put his head in his hands.
Like father, like son!
This was what was going on next door!
Brodie was abusing Jeanette. Blake had seen it all his life and was doing the same.
Deetz went back to the story, reading painfully about the various instances when Blake verbally abused Catherine, intimidated her, gaslighted her, and made her do things that were unspeakable.

After each time, Blake would apologize, break down and cry, and promise to change. He would bring me flowers and gifts with each pathetic apology. Things would get back to normal. We would be happy (as happy as you can be when walking on eggshells). I would hope the past was behind us, the mental torture was over. But then the tension would slowly build between us and the cycle would repeat itself.

The last time I allowed it to happen, it was the middle of the night. He'd not come to bed when I had. He woke me up at 2:30 a.m. and forced me to have relations with him. Then he mocked me and said I was nothing like the kind of women he could find online. I begged him to let me go back to bed; eventually he did. The rest of the night I lay awake planning my escape.

When Blake left for work the next morning, I called my school and told them I had a family emergency and advised them that they would need a substitute teacher, likely through the end of the school year. I threw several suitcases together, took an Uber to the airport, and flew home to my parents' house in Albuquerque. I said nothing to Blake. Needless to say, he was furious.

My father fielded his calls and assured Blake the marriage was over, at least until he got himself fixed. Blake threatened to come out there and get me, but my dad guaranteed him I wasn't going anywhere. My father is an army veteran with a large safe full of firearms. Blake knew not to come anywhere near their home.

I needed time to mend. I began seeing a psychiatrist. The more I spoke with her, the more I realized how drastically and negatively the abusive relationship with Blake had impacted me.

Meanwhile, Blake had gone dark. There was not a peep from him, and it scared me. Although he used to degrade me in his moments of insanity, he was crazy jealous. So, when he went silent, I knew something was going on. I thought perhaps he may take his own life or hire someone to take mine.

Several weeks later my father got a call from Blake. He told my dad he had surrendered his life to Jesus Christ and that he was a new creation. He wanted to see me and explain what had happened. He wanted us to try again.

My dad wasn't having it. I wasn't either—for a while.

But Blake continued to call my dad.

Finally, I told my father I would see Blake, hear him out. He didn't like it but agreed.

Blake flew to Albuquerque and came straight to the house. My dad wouldn't let me go anywhere with him, so we met on the back porch.

Blake looked like a different person.

He'd lost ten pounds. His eyes were bright and clear. His countenance was different—confident yet humble, gentle, kind, and compassionate.

He'd realized the error of his ways and had sought the help of a counselor and then a psychotherapist. With intensive sessions they delved into Blake's childhood, and he came to the realization that his own father had a severe narcissistic personality disorder, a mental health condition in which people have an unreasonably high sense of their own importance.

Deetz was flabbergasted. *Wait till Joanie reads this!* This article was describing Brodie Enoch, his very neighbor! A man who broke into his house and stole his wife's underwear! He glanced at the time on his laptop—expecting Randall Trent at any moment—and continued reading.

Blake realized he had followed in his father's footsteps—seeking too much attention, unsure of his own self-worth, wanting people to admire him, and generally feeling unhappy, unsure, critical, and bitter. Blake also told me he'd taken after his father by being preoccupied with fantasies about power, success, brilliance, beauty, and the perfect mate. In doing so, he sought power over me, calling me names, putting me down, being jealous and possessive, and trying to control me—my spending, what I wore, who I met with, what I ate, and more.

On the porch that day, as Blake spoke to me, he was calm, gentle, and open. He talked to me as he never had before, with the utmost respect. Next, he told me that he knew he couldn't fix himself. The therapist had helped him discover what was wrong, but Blake knew he needed to make drastic changes.

He went on to tell me that he had awoken in the middle of the night

*while we were apart, and something told him to get a Bible. After
searching for twenty minutes, he found one buried in the bottom
cupboard of one of our bookcases. He opened it randomly, pointed,
and started reading: "He himself bore our sins" in his body on the
cross, so that we might die to sins and live for righteousness; "by his
wounds you have been healed." For "you were like sheep going
astray," but now you have returned to the Shepherd and Overseer of
your souls.*

*That one passage of scripture changed Blake's life. He got on his knees
that night and cried out to God to heal him. He found a church that
Sunday. A few weeks later he was baptized. And there he sat on my
parents' porch, virtually begging me to give him another chance.*

"Wayne Deetz," said a deep male voice.

Deetz looked up and there stood big Randall Trent, filling the
doorway in a sopping wet jacket. His face was dark with bruises and
dotted with bandages.

"Sorry," Randall said. "I got here on time but, it took me a
minute to find the conference room."

Deetz closed his laptop, pushed his chair back, and stood.

19

―――――――

"RANDALL TRENT," the man extended a huge hand.

"I remember." Deetz shook his hand.

"Listen, I want to apologize for my behavior at the wedding," Randall said.

Deetz frowned and shook his head, surprised at the man's words.

"Come in and sit down." Deetz took several steps and motioned toward one of the chairs at the long conference room table.

Randall remained where he was. "I can't stay. I just came because you wanted me to. What can I tell you?"

Deetz stood with his hands atop one of the swivel chairs. "What happened to you?" He nodded at Randall's injuries.

"This is the reason Roxanne needs to leave," Randall said. "Bad people are after me. For money I conned out of a widow."

"The widow hired these people?"

Randall nodded. "I'm done with all that. I've made up my mind. But you can't do what I did and not, you know . . ."

Deetz stared at him and waited.

"There are repercussions," Randall said. He motioned toward his battered face. "These are some of the repercussions."

"I've looked at your record," Deetz said. "You've been conning people your whole life. Are you conning me now, telling me your quitting?"

Randall crossed his big arms, looked down, and shook his head. "No, but I can see why you'd think that."

"I've just got to tell you," Deetz said, "I think conning elderly people is despicable. You've made a living at it. I honestly don't know how you sleep at night."

Randall's shoulders lurched as he choked back a wave of emotion. He continued looking down. The room was silent for a long time.

"Look," Randall blurted, "I want to start over. I realize it may be too late. If it is too late, that's on me. I just don't want Roxanne to get dragged into it."

More silence.

"I want to get a job. Just be an average Joe. Take home a paycheck. Blend into the woodwork. I want to give it a go with Roxanne again."

"Does she want that?"

"I think so."

Deetz realized there were hurting people out there whom Randall had swindled, but he also believed the man was genuinely repentant. Of course, he couldn't be sure of that.

Deetz had a chance to be an example, to have some mercy and help the man, but he wasn't sure how.

"What do you want from us?" Deetz said.

"A place for Roxanne to stay, just for a week or so. That's all."

"Where will you be?"

He threw his hands up. "I need to stay at her place. Face the music. I can't keep running. If I can just get this behind me—"

"These are professionals who are after you, correct?"

Randall nodded.

"They'll kill you," Deetz said flatly. "Or cripple you for life."

Randall shook his head and shrugged. "If I run, they'll find me. I need to be done with this."

"How much do you owe?"

Randall squeezed his jaw with a huge hand, the back of which was covered with a thick bandage comprised of white gauze and tape.

"More than I care to tell you."

He looked up at Deetz for a response.

Deetz could only stare at him and sigh, recalling the haunting words from that old Sir Walter Scott poem: *"Oh, what a tangled web we weave when first we practice to deceive."*

"What do you plan on doing when they show up for you?" Deetz said.

Randall shrugged again. "I honestly don't know. Protect myself."

"How do I know they're not going to show up at my house looking for your wife?"

"They know she doesn't have any money. She wasn't part of it. They don't know you or where you live."

"Why don't you just get on a plane and go someplace far away—Cleveland, Baltimore, Miami?"

Randall's eyes grew large. "That's when *they will* go after Roxanne—if I disappear. I'm between a rock and a hard place."

"That you are."

Deetz walked over to the large window and looked out into the wet, cold winter evening. It was Christmastime. They would be having the whole family over. It would be so awkward with Roxanne there. He didn't want her staying at their house, but he also realized nothing happened without it first going through God's hands. As much as Deetz didn't like it, maybe they were supposed to have Roxanne there for some reason. And do so with joy.

"I've got to head out," Randall said.

Deetz turned to face him and said, "Let me think about this some more."

"Fair enough," Randall said. "Thank you for your time." He began to leave, then stuck his head back in as he leaned against the doorframe. "I know you could throw the book at me, and I thank you for not doing that."

Before Deetz could say anything, Randall was gone.

20

———

By the time Deetz got home, Joanie and Leena had finished dinner. Leena was upstairs in her room getting ready for bed and Joanie was wrapping Christmas presents at the island in the kitchen.

Deetz kissed Joanie and said he was starving.

"Chicken Alfredo's in the fridge," she said. "Heat up a plate. There's salad in there, too, if you want it."

"You look beat," Deetz said.

Joanie stopped and stared at him. "I've been busy since I got up this morning. As soon as I finish these I'm going to bed. And by the way, you still haven't told me what you want for Christmas."

Deetz had a plate and was getting things out of the fridge. "I told you, honey, please don't get me anything. I have everything I want. Besides, I haven't gotten you anything."

"Yes you have. Remember?" She laughed. "You got me that leather purse from the Portland Festival of Arts."

"Oh, that's right, the one you bought for yourself. Where is that?"

"I gave it to you."

"Oh, shoot, I better look for that." He put a plate of the pasta in the microwave and started it.

Deetz had told Joanie briefly over the phone on his way home about

106

his visit with Randall. As he ate on a bar stool there at the end of the island, he filled her in on the search he'd done on Brodie and Jeanette Enoch, and their two adult children. He told her all about the magazine story he'd found that was written by their son Blake's wife, Catherine.

"By the looks of it, my guess is the kids don't associate with mom and dad," Deetz said.

"You don't know that for sure," Joanie said.

"No, but they're not friends on social media and the son's wife clearly called Brodie a power-hungry, possessive, controlling jerk. She said he was a severe narcissist."

"I've got to read that," Joanie said.

"I emailed you the link."

There was a loud knock at the door.

Deetz and Joanie looked at each other. It was after 8 p.m. on a freezing December night. Who would be at the door? With all that had been happening lately, Deetz's heart immediately started beating rapidly and Joanie's face fell with a look of concern.

Leena came bopping down the stairs in her robe, pajamas, and moccasins.

Deetz knew she would go straight for the front door.

"Hold on, young lady." Deetz met her in the foyer. "Let me get it."

"Who is it?" Leena said. "I didn't see a car."

"Go in the kitchen with Mom, okay?" Deetz stood and waited for her to go.

"Party pooper," Leena mumbled as she headed for the kitchen.

Deetz went to the window in the dining room and peered over toward the front door.

No.

Brodie and Jeanette Enoch stood there in the cold. He was holding a box wrapped in Christmas paper.

"Who is it?" Leena called.

Deetz just stood there with a gazillion thoughts mixing in his head.

This was getting too weird.

More knocks. Louder this time.

Why don't they use the doorbell?

Joanie stepped into the dining room, tilted her head with a squint, and asked who it was.

"The Enochs," Deetz whispered. "With another present."

Her mouth dropped open and her eyes bulged. Her face darkened. "I can't." She shook her head, turned, and marched back to the kitchen.

That meant he was dealing with it alone. She would stop Leena from coming out there.

God, help me deal with this.

Deetz went into the foyer, took a deep breath, and boldly opened the front door. He purposefully didn't smile.

The cold blasted in.

"Hey neighbor," Brodie said, bouncing on his toes, eyes twitching. "May we come in for a moment? Got a little something for you."

Deetz looked back into the house, unsure what to do, and then back at them.

Should he turn them away cold? Allow them to step inside?

Jeanette was all bundled up with her arms crossed, shivering, wearing a thick red winter hat and a mask covering her nose and mouth. She looked like a ten-year-old child who'd been ordered to go to the neighbors with her dictatorial father.

"We've had a long day," Deetz said. "Believe it or not, I'm about to turn in."

Jeanette suddenly swayed her shoulders as if to say, we should go.

"Come on, Wayne. We'll stay two minutes," Brodie said. "It's freezing out here. Let us inside."

The nerve of this guy!

Jeanette avoided eye contact with Deetz, her eyes zigzagging everywhere but at him.

"Two minutes." Deetz pushed the door open.

Of course, Brodie barged in before his wife, who followed behind him as silently as the dead.

"You want us to take our shoes off?" Brodie said, as if he planned to stay.

Deetz closed the door. "No. Like I said, we're about to turn in for the night."

Jeanette wiped her boots on the rug. Brodie didn't bother.

"Is Joanie here?" Brodie said.

"She's getting ready for bed."

Brodie twitched a smile several times while Jeanette rubbed her red mittened hands together.

"You old folks go to bed early, don't you?" Brodie laughed at his own joke. "That's a shame. Well, here." He handed Deetz the Christmas present, turned toward Jeanette, and said, "Honey . . ."

As if on cue, Jeanette said, "Merry Christmas, from—"

"Take the mask down," Brodie said coldly.

She pulled it down. "Merry Christmas, from our family to yours." All the while her sad eyes searched the ceiling and the rest of the downstairs.

Brodie smiled and nodded and blinked repeatedly. "Any progress on the break-in?"

Jeanette again reacted with the shoulders swaying left and right.

So, he wanted to talk about that? Two could play at Brodie's game. Deetz tossed the Christmas gift up and down in his hands and said, "Another candle?"

"Oh, they opened it!" Brodie said. "Was it a hit?"

Deetz felt his face flush. He glared at the man and told himself not to lose control.

"Oh, wait a second, you're not telling me they took it seriously?" Brodie swung toward Jeanette with an exaggerated look of surprise. "Can you believe that honey?"

Jeanette had not pulled her mask back up and her cheeks broke out in pink blotches.

"It wasn't funny. And it wasn't true," Deetz said.

"Oh, come on," Brodie practically yelled. "It was a joke. And, besides, everyone their age sleeps together. If you don't know that, you're older than I thought you were." He laughed.

Jeanette reached over and brushed Brodie's hand. With the slightest movement she nodded toward the door as if they should leave.

Brodie recoiled.

He seethed and mouthed something to her that must've been nasty, because she looked away as if she'd been burned.

Deetz's heart went out to her.

"You may as well open it," Brodie said.

"I'll wait till Christmas and open it with Joanie," Deetz said, determined to get them out of there. "Thanks for thinking of us." He walked the few steps to the front door and began to open it.

"Boy, you are not subtle at all, Wayne. Wow." Brodie crossed to the door. "I thought you were some devout Christian, but you are downright nasty. I thought we were supposed to know you Christians by your love. Come on, Jeanette. We can only try so hard."

Brodie grabbed Jeanette's hand and barged out into the cold night.

Deetz shut the door and stood there holding the present.

"What was that?" Joanie said, stepping into the dining room.

Leena followed, holding an ice cream bar.

"Honey," Deetz said to her, "why don't you turn in now. Mom and I need to talk."

Leena took a bite of the ice cream. "Can't we open that gift before I go up?" she pleaded.

Joanie nixed that. "No, Leena. Time for bed. Dad and I need some time together before we go to bed."

"Good night," Leena said in a defeated tone, before giving each of them a peck on the cheek and heading for the stairs. "I am an adult, you know. And I should probably be included in these secret talks about the neighbors. You're missing some invaluable insights."

"Sleep tight," Deetz said. Then he whispered to Joanie, "Let's go in the den."

Once they were seated next to each other on the couch with the Christmas present from the Enoch's on the table in front of them, Wayne asked if Joanie had heard everything. She said she had.

"You should have seen Jeanette," he said. "I honestly believe he's abusing her—mentally at the very least."

"I don't even want to know what's in there," Joanie said, nodding toward the gift.

"The thing is, he knows I'm police," Deetz said. "Why would he dare come over here?"

"He's crazy, that's why."

"How does he know I'm a Christian?" Deetz said. "We've never talked about that."

"Because he's stalking you. And me, I'm sure," Joanie said.

"He probably has a chip on his shoulder toward Christians because his son and daughter-in-law got saved."

"We need to open that," Joanie eyed the gift, but continued sitting slumped back on the couch.

Deetz leaned forward and picked up the box. He untied the ribbon and ripped the red and green and white wrapping paper away, crunched it up, and tossed it onto the table.

The box was white, about twelve inches by twelve inches, and two inches deep. It was taped closed. Deetz got his pocketknife out and slit the three spots where it had been taped.

"Hurry up," Joanie said.

Deetz opened the lid and pushed aside the white tissue.

He sat still and stared.

It was a framed photograph of their own house all lit up at night.

"Well?" Joanie said.

The eight-by-ten photograph was taken from the Deetz's front yard. Spindly tree branches crept into the top edge of the picture. Several lights were on downstairs and upstairs in Leena's room.

Without a word, Deetz handed the box to Joanie.

He was trying to figure out when the picture had been taken, and why. Why would Brodie give them this?

Joanie got it out of the box. The frame was nice—thick, rustic brown stained wood. She turned it over. There was a note taped on the back. She read it aloud: "Always watching! Love, Brodie & Jeanette."

"This is just cryptic," Joanie said, tossing it onto the couch.

Deetz picked it up, read the note, and examined the picture again.

"He was out there," Joanie pointed toward the front yard, "at night, watching our house. Look at Leena's room—all lit up. He's a *stalker*. Can you arrest him for that? Stalking? Trespassing? I cannot believe this."

Deetz just sat there shaking his head in a daze of disbelief.

"Wayne?"

"No. I mean, even if we could arrest him on something like that, he'd be in and out in no time. We need to nail him on bigger charges. Burglary. Home invasion. Spousal abuse. Domestic violence."

"We're throwing that out," Joanie said, pointing at the picture.

"I need to keep it. For evidence. Don't worry. I'll hide it."

Joanie got up and retrieved her laptop. "I've got to read that story the daughter-in-law wrote."

"Oh boy. Here we go."

21

THE LAST SEVERAL weeks of December were always chaotic at the Portland Police Bureau and throughout the city, and this Tuesday morning had proven no different. Lots of employees wanted to take time off for Christmas and New Year's, yet more staff was needed over the holidays—which always produced a variety of wacky family disputes, robberies, DUIs, and thefts.

Deetz poured a steaming cup of coffee from his thermos in the conference room and looked over the gray city of Portland. Cold and misty, as usual. He got an eerie chill as that awful day of the mass shooting on Pioneer Square came back to haunt him, and his interrogations of the teenage shooter, Rogan Sneed. Here it was seven years later, and the event still disturbed Deetz to the core every day.

He looked at the date on his watch and counted—ten more days till he was done.

It was difficult to believe.

He and Joanie were entering a new phase of life. Really, the final chapter.

God had blessed him in that job for thirty-five years. Kept him safe *all that time*. Deetz was beyond grateful and knew it was only by God's hand that he'd survived. "Ten more days, Lord," he whispered.

He would miss the camaraderie of working with the honorable

men and women who had become his closest friends, but he would not miss the often-unspeakable crimes he would have to investigate, nor the devastating fallout they would inevitably leave in their wake.

Joanie was going to be so relieved. He looked forward to—

Two knocks at the door and Howard Googan rolled in with a huge cup of coffee, a small box of donuts, and his walloping backpack. "Morning, Deetz."

"Morning, Googan." Deetz noticed he was only three minutes late and he could still smell the cold on him.

Googan opened the box and slid it over to Deetz. "Donut?"

"Emm. I will. Thanks." Deetz took a bite of a powdered and watched Googan get out of his huge coat and get his big laptop set up. Everything about this guy was large and in charge.

"So, last night I talked to a guy at a hole in the wall called the Golden Pole Barn down around the docks. He's a regular there. Everyone at the club knows him. He told me he's a friend of Regina Hart's—a.k.a. Dawn Delight. It turns out Regina confided to him that one of the patrons there had been following her from club to club for the last few months. It creeped her out."

Deetz ate his donut with his coffee, listening with interest.

"You with me?" Googan said.

"All ears. Great work."

"Glad you approve. So, Regina described this person of interest to this regular and the regular thinks he knows who the guy is. Doesn't know his name but would recognize him. Oh, and he's been known to show up at these clubs with a woman, occasionally —a wife or partner. But, get this, the person of interest hasn't been back ever since Regina disappeared."

Deetz was impressed.

"I told you about the male dancer there," Googan said. "He's promised to call me if and when the person of interest shows up again; same with the regular."

"You aren't afraid to put in the hours, are you?"

"Now that I'm divorced, this is all I have. So yeah. It keeps me busy."

"So, what's next on this?"

"I've got a computer artist from our team meeting with the

friend of Regina's at the Golden Pole Barn. He'll do a composite sketch of the guy. Since this is an abduction—"

"We're not positive of that."

"Deetz, please, trust me on this. I know an abduction when I see one. I want to get the sketch out to other agencies at least statewide. Also, post it on all our social media sites. Good?"

Deetz thought it through and decided to trust Googan's instincts. "Okay, run with it."

Googan nodded, closed his laptop, and got to his feet. "You also wanted to go over that daily checklist with me at some point."

"Oh, right. Do you have time now?"

Googan looked at his watch and there was a knock at the door.

Both men looked that way.

It was Deetz's son, Brandon, and his police partner and best friend, Clarence Waters, both in uniform and looking sharp.

"Hey Dad," Brandon said.

"Hey, Investigator Deetz," said Clarence.

Deetz introduced the boys to Howard Googan, who excused himself, saying he had to meet up with the composite sketch artist. He and Deetz agreed to catch up later.

When Googan was gone, Deetz asked what the boys were up to.

"We just brought in a porch pirate," Brandon said. "He was following an Amazon driver all morning, filling his minivan with packages."

"You should have seen this dude's van," Clarence said. "It was *packed* from the front seat to the back door. Floor to ceiling."

"Who tipped off the driver?" Deetz said.

"He finally noticed he was being followed and called us," Brandon said. "Anyway, you've heard about Roxanne?"

"Yeah. Randall was just here, not too long ago," Deetz said.

"That's what Mom said," Brandon said in an irritated tone. "What's going on?"

Deetz explained everything and told Brandon that he and Joanie were probably going to invite Roxanne to stay at the house.

"That's insane, Dad. Why?"

"You don't want her staying with you and Kristen, do you?" Deetz chuckled and so did Clarence.

"No, but you guys are too old for that. And during Christmas? I feel like it's my fault." "No, it's Randall's fault, but like I told you, he's trying to turn over a new leaf."

"But what are those people going to do to him?" Clarence said. "How's he going to get out of that mess?"

"Well, that's the problem," Deetz said. "I don't have an answer. I'm still thinking about what can be done, if anything."

"Kristen feels awful. She's so embarrassed," Brandon said. "I can't believe you're helping that guy. Are you sure he's not just using you?"

"Son, he and Roxanne sound like they're trying to make things right. Start over. He's very remorseful. Your mom and I will help if we can. Who else is going to help them?"

Brandon sighed. "You're a better man than me."

"Me, too," said Clarence.

"How's the new guy working out?" Brandon said, nodding toward the door where Googan had exited.

"Not bad. We started out on the wrong foot, but he knows what he's doing. He'll be fine, I'm sure. We all think we're irreplaceable, but we're not."

"How are you feeling about retiring Mr. Deetz?" Clarence asked.

Deetz shook his head and threw his hands up. "I'm ready, I guess." He chuckled. "Joanie's ready. We'll see. After all these years it's going to be really different. But I plan to stay busy."

Deetz's phone vibrated and he reached for it.

"What's the latest on that nut-job next door?" Brandon said.

Deetz looked at his phone. "It's your mom. Let me take this."

"Okay. We're out, Dad. Later."

"Later, Mr. Deetz."

Deetz waved them goodbye and answered the call.

"Wayne, can you come home?" Joanie's voice was frantic; she was out of breath. "I found something you need to see. You need to *hurry.*"

"Honey, okay, slow down. What is it? What did you find?"

"It's some kind of . . . device. It's small and black and it's like a camera or a recorder. I bet you anything Brodie Enoch did this when he broke in."

"Where? Where did you find it?"

"I was vacuuming, in our room. I hit the bed and it dropped to the floor. Can you please come?"

"I'm on my way."

22

Joanie and Wayne had talked again on his way home and he
had suggested they not speak within the vicinity of the device when
he got there, in case it was indeed a microphone or bug of some
kind. He also told her to handle it as little as possible in case it
contained someone's fingerprints.

When he first got home, Joanie had met Wayne with the
device, which she carried in a paper towel. He examined it, set it
down, and led her into the walk-in pantry in the kitchen. He whispered, "There's not an on/off switch so it may have to be turned
on and off with an app on a phone or a computer. Let me look
online to see if I can find it." He put an index finger to his lips.
"Shhh."

Joanie followed him into the kitchen and counted back to the
evening of Brandon's wedding and the break-in at their house and
figured it had been ten days. If it was planted under the bed that
long ago, could it still be holding a charge? They weren't sure if the
device still had power because there was no light on it. It did have a
tiny micro-port which Joanie assumed was for charging it.

Wayne sat on a barstool at the kitchen island with the device
sitting next to his laptop as he searched online to try to find out
exactly what it was. She was a nervous wreck and was just looking
for something to do to waste time. She whispered, "Have you
eaten?"

"I'm fine," he said, totally zeroed in on the task at hand. He likely had not eaten.

Joanie examined the device, which was only the size of a matchbox. It was made of black plastic and metal, and had a small area of grooves on one side that made it look like a speaker or microphone.

After a few minutes, Deetz leaned back on the barstool, sighed, and pointed at the screen on his laptop. She came and peered over his shoulder. The device he had found online was almost exactly like the device sitting in front of them. It was called the Super Mini Spy Listening Unit.

Joanie got dizzy when those words sunk in.

She slowly read the description, gripping Wayne's shoulder as she did. "Light weight, easy to carry and hide . . . Simply call the SIM number installed in the unit and hear voices within ten meters . . . Voice-activated to save battery life . . . No power light so the unit remains discreet . . . Exceptional sound quality makes spying pinpoint accurate . . . One charge can last up to 14 days."

Chills engulfed Joanie's entire body.

They looked at each other soberly.

Deetz didn't know how far ten meters was so he opened another screen on the laptop and quickly found a meter calculator; ten meters equaled 32.8 feet, which was supposedly how far the mini spy unit could pick up voices.

Joanie's face burned with anger, and embarrassment.

Someone—most probably Brodie Enoch—had been listening to everything that went on in their bedroom, and possibly into their bathroom and even into the family room, for the past ten days.

Deetz stood, snatched the device within the paper towel, and took it into their bedroom, and on into the bathroom, where he left it. He exited, shut that door, came back through the bedroom and shut that door. He shook his head as he led her back into the kitchen. She could tell he was fuming.

"I'm going to take it into headquarters and have them look at it," he said. "It probably won't have prints on it, but they'll be able to tell me more, I hope. If it does have a SIM card, maybe they can trace it. I'm not sure. I've never seen one of these."

Joanie stuck her hands on her waist. "This is making me sick, Wayne."

A tide of emotion welled up in her and she began to cry.

Deetz gathered her into his arms. He held her close.

"Don't you worry about this, honey. I'll take care of it. I'm not going to let anything happen to you."

She pulled back and looked at him, her face cold and wet with tears. "Think about all he heard!"

She cried harder.

Wayne embraced her again and the room fell silent.

"Father in heaven," he prayed, "we don't know why this is happening, but we ask you to intervene, to stop this . . . whatever it is. *Please.* Give us wisdom about what to do. Protect us. Protect our privacy. Protect us from evil. Put your angels all around this house, around us and our family. Keep us safe and at peace. Expose this thing, now, please."

After a moment of silence, Joanie whispered, "Amen."

Wayne squeezed her one last time.

They looked into each other's eyes. Both nodded.

"I've got to get back to work," he said. "Let me grab that thing."

He headed off to get the device.

Joanie wandered into the dining room and looked out at the front yard and quiet street.

Amazingly, it wasn't raining. The sky was white. It was cold outside, probably about forty degrees.

Out the corner of her eye, toward the Enoch place, a large camper van slowly backed out of the driveway.

The hair on the back of Joanie's neck stood straight up.

Brodie was driving and no one was in the passenger seat.

"Wayne!" Joanie yelled, not taking her eyes off it. "Come, quick. The camper!"

She heard him coming and made herself focus hard on what the vehicle looked like.

White. Maybe twenty feet long. It looked like a modern van but on steroids—longer, taller.

Brodie glanced toward the window where Joanie stood, and she leaned back.

Wayne got to the window just as the vehicle backed out of the driveway and into the street.

It had two tinted sliding windows on the side Joanie could see, with two long horizontal black stripes. On top it looked like there was a sunroof, a solar panel, and some other equipment.

The camper van stopped in the street, its exhaust visible and churning out the tailpipe.

Wayne had his phone out. He held it up and snapped several pictures, not caring if Brodie saw him.

Brodie put it in Drive and slowly pulled away, taking one last glance back at the window where Joanie and Wayne stood.

"I'm going to try to follow him," Wayne said, turning away, grabbing his coat and keys.

Good, Joanie thought. *While you're doing that, I have an idea of my own. All I need is an excuse to show up at the Enoch's door.*

23

Deetz made it to the Subaru quickly but didn't know whether he'd be able to catch up with Brodie or not. The camper van looked like a newer model, sleek and streamlined, not like some cumbersome old motor home. Deetz backed out of the driveway in a hurry and noticed Brodie's Jeep was not in the Enoch's driveway. Deetz zipped through the neighborhood much faster than he should. When he came to a stop at the main entrance of the subdivision, he looked right and didn't see Brodie, then left.

There!

The white camper van stood out from the other vehicles on the four-lane road due to its height; it was cruising west on Inverness Boulevard, about a half-mile off.

Deetz waited until it was clear and took off after it.

His phone buzzed. He peeked at the screen. It was a mug shot sketch of a white male, mid-forties, thin, glasses, day-old beard growth. The sketches these days were all created on computers, so they all featured the harsh black pencil markings on stark white backgrounds. To be honest, a lot of them looked the same.

Deetz was in the left lane catching up to the white camper van. Once he got within several hundred yards, he dropped back over into the right lane with other cars between them.

Deetz glanced at the sketch again and thumbed upward. It was indeed the 'Person of Interest' alert from Howard Googan, sent out to all police agencies throughout Oregon. The message was concise yet informative. Deetz shook his head, amazed at how fast Googan got that done. He had to snicker. After thirty-five years in law enforcement, Deetz thought he was quite good at what he did, rather an expert. Yet, here came Howard Googan, probably every bit as talented. *There's always someone waiting in line to replace you.*

JOANIE'S HEART raced as she stood staring out the dining room window at the wet front yard. With Wayne and Brodie gone it was her chance to dash over and to try to talk to Jeanette. With every fiber of her being, Joanie felt Jeanette was in trouble and was, at the very least, being mentally abused by Brodie Enoch. She also knew Jeanette probably held the answers to the break-in at their home, the missing things, and the listening device.

Joanie got her parka out of the hall closet and put it on, thinking about what she would say to Jeanette. She did not know.

Lord, give me the words. Help us connect. Bring out the truth.

As she left the house and headed through the yard toward the Enoch house, she rolled her shoulders, then her neck, forcing herself to relax, to breathe deeply. With each step she realized how scared she was of Brodie. If he were to return home while she was there, she feared what he would do to her.

She blocked from her mind how upset Wayne would be if he knew what she was doing.

She got to the driveway, hurried up the sidewalk to the front door, and rang the doorbell without hesitation. *No turning back now.*

Brodie's Jeep was gone, and the garage door was down, but Joanie could see Jeanette's car through the garage window. She rang the doorbell again.

Come on.

Jeanette was so quiet, she could be right there at the door looking at Joanie through the peephole.

Joanie knocked loudly. "Jeanette, it's Joanie. I know you're home. I just want to talk."

Surprisingly, the door nudged open.

Only five inches.

Jeanette wore a gray mask. Her dull eyes were sunk in her head. What could be seen of her face was pasty white.

A black cat whirled around at the foot of the door and Jeanette gently pushed it back into the house with her foot.

"I can't talk," she mumbled softly as she peeked out through the small opening, the interior of the house black behind her.

"Why not? Just for a minute. I know Brodie's gone."

Jeanette's eyes shifted up to a corner of the front porch. Joanie followed her gaze up to where a small camera pointed down at them.

Joanie looked back at her and whispered, "I'll come inside."

Jeanette blinked and shook her head once, concisely. She pulled the mask down below her chin. "There are cameras inside, too," she whispered. "I have to go. Really."

Joanie leaned close. "Is he hurting you? Wayne is police. Just tell me and it's over."

Suddenly, tears welled up in Jeanette's eyes. Her mouth hung open and her bottom lip quivered as if she wanted to speak. But she looked hyper alert, as if Brodie was standing right inside the door beside her.

"The lady—Joanie Deetz!" For a second Joanie was confused.

The male voice came from someplace on the front porch and sounded like an old portable transistor radio.

Jeanette's eyes—only her eyes—shot up toward the camera.

"What is it you need, neighbor?" came Brodie's voice—from the camera! "I can hear you. You can say hi. And tell me what you're doing at our house on this fine day."

The moment was so surreal, Joanie got light-headed and put a hand on the doorframe to steady herself. As things came into focus, she realized that Brodie—*while driving that camper*—must be watching from an app on his phone.

Who does this?!

"Say something," Jeanette whispered as if giving advice on how to pacify Brodie.

"Uh," Joanie looked at Jeanette a second longer, then back up at the camera. "Hello. Just here to borrow two eggs."

"Oh? Are we still friends?" Brodie said. "After the absurd accusations?"

Jeanette said shyly, "Let me go get those eggs for you." The door closed.

Joanie slowly turned and looked back up at the camera.

"I see Jeanette's playing along with your game," Brodie said in transistor voice. "That's not good, Joanie. You're proving to be a bad influence on her. I need you to stay away from our house. Do you understand me? We tried to be nice—*very* nice. But you've proven to be nothing but nasty."

Joanie was frozen in place, sorting through several ways she could respond. Finally, she settled on lying to him.

"If you're saying something I can't understand you. It's just static. I only got bits and pieces of that." She turned back around to face the closed door.

Brodie cussed loudly.

Wait till Joanie told Wayne about this. He's not going to believe it.

"No one is allowed to talk to Jeanette when I'm not there," Brodie's tinny voice yelled from the tiny camera speaker.

Joanie did not move, wanting it to seem like she had not heard anything.

"In fact, if you and your family don't stay out of our business, there will be consequences."

It took everything in Joanie not to turn and face the camera and give Brodie a piece of her mind.

The door opened.

Thank God.

Jeanette eyed Joanie, then, with spindly white fingers, handed her two eggs and slowly looked back up at the camera.

"Yes, I'm still watching you, Jeanette Enoch," Brodie said harshly.

Joanie swung around and looked up at the camera. "It's all static. We can't understand a word you're saying."

"I need to go," Jeanette said.

"Are you being hurt?" Joanie whispered, desperately.

"Joanie, you need to go!" Brodie screamed through the little speaker.

Jeanette's nostril flared. Her eyes glistened as she took one last glance at Joanie and closed the door.

24

———————

WHAT DID that Joanie Deetz think, that Brodie couldn't hear her asking Jeanette if she was being hurt by him? And for Joanie to try to tell him that she couldn't understand what he was saying, static—that was a lie! That camera was the best money could buy. She'd heard him. That nosy wench was going to pay for meddling in the Enoch's business. And Jeanette never should have answered the door. She was going to have some explaining to do when he got home.

Brodie steamed and cursed a blue streak. He closed the camera app and tossed his phone into a cupholder on the console. He looked at his watch and figured he was twenty more minutes away from the campsite. He glanced back at his passenger who was lying on the bed in the back with her hands zip-tied to a metal handle he'd had custom-made solely for this purpose. She'd learned by now not to cry and scream while they were driving. It did her no good. Much like the others had learned.

As he cruised along carefully at the speed limit in the right lane, he checked his rearview mirror and wondered for the hundredth time if kidnapping Joanie Deetz would be worth the risk. Oh, it would be an amazing head-rush, that was for sure. But he tried never to make these things personal. He'd never taken anyone he actually knew. That would be taking the risk to the next level. So, that would be a new one. Chancy, but oh-so-rewarding. He would have to ponder it. Boy, would that throw old Deetz into a tizzy. *Ha!*

He glanced back again at sweet Dawn. She'd lost weight. He needed to do a better job of feeding her. She had access to plenty of water, that was the main thing. He realized with this one he had to be especially careful. She was smart. If he ever put his guard down with this one, she would be gone.

He drove along in silence.

It had been bold of Jeanette to answer the door when Joanie came over. Too bold. A year ago, she never would have done such a thing. Brodie wondered if she saw hope for freedom in the Deetzes. It would be understandable. Wayne was gutsy coming to the door with his sergeant, searching the place. Perhaps the gifts Brodie had given them had been too over-the-top. But that was part of the thrill for him. He delighted in shocking others, making people take notice of him, having control, and causing people to wonder—who is this Brodie Enoch?

He heard slurping and turned around. She was drinking from the plastic water bottle he always made sure was close-by. She drank, awkwardly with her hands tied, and then stopped suddenly and looked at him. Oh, if looks could kill old Brodie would be dead. She was strong, this one. And not as afraid as he liked. His face twitched involuntarily.

He looked back and she did the same.

She mimicked his twitch!

His head swiveled back to the road in front of him and he searched frantically for the first place he could pull over and teach her a lesson!

There!

A Wendy's.

He hit the blinker and swung into the parking lot.

It was well after the lunchtime rush, so the front parking lot was empty except for a small car and a large heating and A/C truck.

Good.

He rolled to the back of the parking lot where only two cars were parked. He turned the camper van around and backed in against a row of thick bushes, so he was facing the restaurant and street. He threw it in Park, whirled around from the leather captain's chair, and headed back toward the woman on the bed.

"What have I told you about mimicking me?" he barked.

By the time he got to her, she had her knees folded up against her chest in defense as she lay on her back.

"Huh?" he barked. "What have I told you?"

He got madder with each second and went for her with both hands to throttle her neck, and her legs sprung and bashed him in the chest. Then her legs folded up to her chest again in the same defensive position.

She'd not said a word and wore a look of feisty determination beneath the bruises and red welts on her lovely face.

"Why you!" He clenched his teeth and hissed. Her defense made him even angrier. "Who do you think you are?"

He lunged at her and she smashed him again with a squeal this time and recoiled again.

He grabbed her ankles and yanked her half off the bed until her arms were outstretched way above her head, and her hands were being strangled by the zip-ties.

"Ahhh!" she screamed.

"Shush! Shut it!"

She yelled as loud as she could, her face red, the thin bones in her neck protruding.

Brodie threw her ankles to the floor and went for the Chloroform in the drawer by the built-in desk. Hands trembling, he dumped some onto a red bandana and marched it back to her.

Her eyes bulged and she screamed and backed up as far as she could onto the bed. She'd had this treatment before and knew what was coming.

"I will teach you to mimic me, and to scream like a banshee." He batted her flying knees away and smothered her mouth with the bandana. She struggled and fought and kicked and raged for a good sixty seconds. Then her body finally fell limp.

Brodie dropped to the floor, exhausted from battling her.

She was strong—and determined.

He caught his breath.

This one was getting too bold.

He felt something burning on his right wrist and looked. A long, bleeding gash where she'd dug her nails into him.

He cursed and wiped the sweat from his forehead.

She was getting much more daring. She was feeling the desperation. He was beginning to worry that she might figure out a way to escape when he left her this time. Perhaps he should move up the timetable to dispose of her.

Why risk keeping her alive?

He got to his knees, then stood up with a grunt and looked down at her.

A beautiful creature.

But, yes, it may be time to say their goodbyes.

He got some paper towels from the little kitchen, wet it at the sink, and pressed it against the cut on his wrist. Thinking. Thinking. Thinking.

The plan *had been* to leave her at the campground for another night or two, and to bring her back to the house for one final round of fun. The campsite he'd secured was fairly far from other campers, and it backed up to a busy highway. No one could hear her. But still, *if* she found a way to escape, he'd be finished. And he wasn't ready to be finished. Yes, he knew that time would come. But not yet.

He took one last look at the woman, retrieved a Slim Jim from a narrow cabinet at the kitchen, and went forward, plunking down into the comfy driver's seat. He swung back around to face forward, opened the Slim Jim, took a bite, and debated his next move.

Several cars lined up at the drive-thru now.

Two teenage girls walked into the restaurant without a clue that a killer was watching them.

To get rid of sweet Dawn would require a trip.

Jeanette would need to come with him, because he would require her help, and because he didn't want to leave her at the house alone anymore.

He needed to think this through.

The driver at the drive-thru was handed a Frosty.

Yum.

He loved those things.

He would go in and buy one and figure out a plan. Mustn't rush this. He tossed the half-eaten Slim Jim onto the console, opened the driver's door, glanced back at sleeping Dawn, and jumped down from the driver's seat onto the wet blacktop.

He locked the camper and bundled up as he crossed the parking lot.

No . . . it can't be.

Uh oh.

Wayne Deetz!

A wave of heat hit Brodie in the face, and he slowed down and cursed under his breath. But he made the split-second decision to keep walking, go inside, figure this out.

Don't panic.

Once inside, he kept an eye on Deetz's Subaru, parked at the McDonald's across the street, to make sure the old man didn't leave the car and start to come his way. Brodie kept looking back as he placed his order.

This was confirmation. The old blood hound was on Brodie's scent.

This is real.

But it seemed *surreal*, because Brodie had never been searched, suspected, and followed like this before. The heat was on, and it rather thrilled him.

There were only three other patrons in the Wendy's—the two girls he'd watched walk in and a man wearing grungy navy work pants and a matching navy coat with a heating and air logo on back.

The unkempt young man in the untucked uniform handed him the Frosty and a spoon. With an eye on the Subaru, Brodie opened the plastic wrap around the spoon, removed the lid from the cup, and began eating.

He walked toward the tinted front window of the restaurant and looked across the street at Deetz who was seated low in the driver's seat, wearing sunglasses.

Brodie could try to lose him, but that wasn't a good option in the camper van.

Oh no. Ugh. Brain-freeze. Too much Frosty too quickly. *Slow down.*

He could drive back to the house, but that would be precarious, especially with Deetz so hot on his trail. Or he could just march right over there and confront Deetz, threaten him to stay away. But what good would that do? Deetz would probably still follow him. No, Brodie needed to figure out a way to disable Deetz's vehicle, or to get him called away from there altogether.

25

Deetz had Joanie on speaker phone while he watched the Wendy's across the street, waiting for Brodie Enoch to get back in his camper van. With each passing minute, this thing with the Enochs got stranger. Joanie had just finished telling him that she had visited the Enoch's house—over which he totally blew a gasket—and that Brodie had been *watching* her interaction with Jeanette at the front door via the security camera at the top corner of the porch. He had even *talked* to Joanie through the camera somehow. And he did it all on his phone while driving the camper van as Deetz followed him.

It was so bizarre that Deetz was getting those eerie—and frankly, scary—feelings he usually got when tracking a psychopath.

Anything could happen—to anyone.

And it didn't help that the Deetz house was in such close proximity to the Enoch house.

But right now, Deetz didn't have anything solid on Brodie, and he didn't have a lot more time to follow the camper van. He had to get back to police headquarters and he wanted to get that listening device to the tech team. But, in Deetz's mind, something about Brodie and that camper van did not sit well—at all.

"Wayne?" Joanie said.

"Sorry, honey. My mind was drifting. What did you say?"

"Roxanne accepted our invitation. She's coming tomorrow."

Deetz closed his eyes and told himself not to say anything derogatory.

"I'm going to make Brandon's room up for her," Joanie said. "Not now. I'll do it in the morning."

"Ho, ho, ho," Deetz said. "The more the merrier."

"I'm also planning out the menu for Christmas and I'm going to need your help—"

The side door at Wendy's swung open. It was Brodie.

"Here he is!" Deetz sat up and watched as Brodie sauntered across the parking lot. "Let me go, honey. I'll talk to you soon."

"Okay. Be careful, Wayne. I love you."

"Love you."

Brodie held a cup in one hand and stuffed the other in his coat pocket as he walked back toward the camper van, seemingly in no hurry.

The door to Wendy's opened again and a husky man in a dark blue work uniform exited and headed toward a company truck not far away. He hopped in and the truck rumbled to life with a big cloud of exhaust.

Brodie got in the camper van, crouched, and disappeared toward the back.

The heating and A/C truck backed up, then forward, and bumped out of the lot like the guy was in a hurry. But then the truck lurched several times and the driver put his blinker on and merged into the center turn lane.

Brodie reappeared, plopped into the driver's seat, and started the camper van.

Deetz checked his watch and was anxious to follow further. If Brodie were to park the camper van wherever he'd left the Jeep, and then took the Jeep back home, it would give Deetz a chance to search the camper and campsite.

Brodie put the camper van in Drive and slowly began rolling out of the lot.

Something caught the corner of Deetz's eye.

The huge orange and blue heating and A/C truck eased up slowly right behind Deetz—and stopped!

Deetz checked his rear-view mirror, and the blasted truck seemed inches from his rear bumper.

What the . . .

Deetz busted out of his car and ran back to the big box truck, which was stopped three feet from his bumper. The driver's window slowly cranked down.

"I'm sorry, fella," a man with curly red hair stuck his head out the window. "She does this sometimes. Right when I got on the road she started chokin' and spittin'. That's why I pulled over. Don't worry. I'll get 'er goin'."

"Hurry!" Deetz yelled. "I'm police. I need to get out—now!"

Could Brodie have paid this guy?

Deetz looked over as Brodie eased the camper van to a stop at the main highway right across the street.

Deetz stepped behind the box truck so Brodie wouldn't see him.

The engine of the box truck cranked, but it wouldn't turn over. It cranked again and stopped.

Deetz eyed the front of his car for a way out forward, but it was completely blocked in by a concrete bumper and, ahead of that, a twelve-foot drainage swale that ran horizontal with the highway.

The truck cranked again but fell silent. The driver cursed.

Deetz heard the hood of the truck pop open, and the driver opened his door and began to climb out.

Brodie had his right blinker on and merged out onto the highway.

"Can we roll it out of my way?" Deetz said, anxiously. "I need to get out now!"

"We can't push this thing, bud. It weighs fourteen thousand pounds," said the tall, burly driver with a ruddy face. "But I know what to do. Just give me another minute or two."

As Brodie pulled away and began to accelerate eastbound, he honked the horn three times, and soon the camper van was a speck on the horizon.

Deetz seethed as the driver slammed the hood shut and rambled back up into the driver's seat.

"Let me guess," Deetz called up to him. "That guy in the camper paid you to do this."

The truck cranked and rumbled to life. The driver gave it gas, revved the engine, and the truck shook.

"No sir," the driver glanced down at Deetz, who heard it shift gears. "But I'm out of your way now. Sorry about that and have a blessed day."

"You could be arrested for accessory; do you realize that?" Deetz yelled as the truck chugged away.

Deetz stood there with his hands on his waist and looked down the highway in the direction Brodie had gone, making a mental note of it.

His shoulders dropped and he sighed.

He got into his car with a groan and started it up.

Just then, the big orange and blue box truck chugged by on the highway right in front of him, almost mocking him. As Deetz backed up and put the Subaru in Drive, he could have sworn the truck driver saluted him.

26

———

JEANETTE ENOCH SAT IN HER "SAFE" chair in the corner by the window overlooking the backyard. She couldn't see anything out there now because it was dark—dark, cold, wet, and windy. The golden glow of the lamp from the table beside her reflected in the window and shone down on the purple and white blanket she was knitting.

Brodie would be home soon, she guessed. She had no way of knowing where he was because he always hid her phone when he went somewhere, and she dare not look for it. He had cameras everywhere throughout the house and could see every move she made; even the hallways and bathrooms had cameras.

She called this her "safe" chair because, when she sat in it, he couldn't sneak up behind her because it was situated in the corner. She was surprised he hadn't figured that out by now and moved it someplace else.

She continued knitting, knowing that at least one of Brodie's small cameras was trained on her now. She knew that because of the time not long after they'd moved in she'd brought a cookie to the chair to eat after lunch. She'd enjoyed it so much that she went and got another. When she plopped back down in the chair and began to eat it, Brodie's voice came over the camera speaker, scaring her half to death and chastising her for indulging in too many sweets.

As she sat there now, Jeanette felt a ball of dread spinning in her stomach. She forced herself to continue knitting and tried to relax. Would Brodie discipline her for opening the door to Joanie Deetz that afternoon? Or perhaps her lie had worked, about Joanie coming over to borrow the two eggs. She didn't know. But she did know that, for Brodie to speak out over the camera as he had to Joanie, well, her visit had rattled him.

The neighbors were indeed getting closer and closer to figuring out that something horribly wrong was taking place in the Enoch household.

And where was Brodie now?

Probably taking that poor woman, Dawn, back to the campsite and bringing the Jeep home. He'd implied that he would be bringing her back again one or two more times. And then what? Jeanette got slightly dizzy. She would never see the woman again, as with the others.

In slow motion, memories of Brodie's demented and torturous behavior threatened to creep into Jeanette's mind—memories of Dawn, and other women, in other towns, in other houses—but she forced the disquieting recollections down and out and away. Away. Away. *Away.*

She purposefully turned her focus to better things, cleaner things, purer things—to the row she was knitting and to whom she might gift the blanket; to the only friends she had, her cats, JoJo and Danny; to her plants and flowers and how much they loved this rain.

Then, on a dime, her thoughts spun to Joanie Deetz, Wayne Deetz, and that huge Sergeant Tidwell; to how close they had come to catching a demented man; her slave master; a killer.

With the camera on her, knowing Brodie was checking it, she was scared he may somehow read her thoughts and see the tiny ember of hope hidden away, but glowing dimly deep in her soul. It was something she hadn't felt for all the years they'd been married.

From day one he had turned into a monster, and the joyful, hopeful woman she had once been had been suffocated. He was impulsive and had an insatiable need for control. Jeanette had researched his characteristics and found him to be a true psychopath—a predator who could use charm, manipulation, intimidation, and violence to satisfy his own selfish desires.

Another piece of research she'd found, which she'd memorized, fit Brodie perfectly as well: socially maladjusted, sudden outbursts, strong need for passive affection and attention, sexual conflict suggestive of sadomasochism, and irrational and impulsive behavior.

Jeanette knew nothing of God. But she did know Brodie hated that the Deetzes were what he repeatedly called, "delusional Christians." Could it be that God had directed her and Brodie to move next-door to a veteran police investigator?

The thought of it made her heart soar and tears flooded her eyes without warning. She ripped her head away from the wall with the camera and pretended to look out the window. Discreetly, she wiped the tears away with the sleeve of her baggy sweatshirt.

JoJo, the black cat, surprised Jeanette, jumping up into her lap. She stroked him but quickly pushed him back down to the floor, knowing Brodie couldn't stand it when the cats got on the furniture. Any trace of hair on the chairs and he would totally lose his cool, sometimes throwing the cats across the room.

Jeanette thought back to Joanie's visit that day. Jeanette had come within inches of writing an SOS message on a tiny piece of paper and handing it to Joanie with the two eggs, but she was afraid Joanie would have reacted strangely, and Brodie would have seen it over his video feed.

After running into Joanie at the Portland Plaza of Shoppes—the day Brodie had forced Jeanette to wear Joanie's dress and shoes and underwear—Brodie had gathered everything up that he'd taken from the Deetz's house in a large black trash bag and took it with him the next time he left in his Jeep.

If only Deetz and Tidwell had searched Brodie's computers.

They would have found everything.

Video recordings of how he mentally and physically tortured her.

And the other women, in the other towns, in the other houses.

Jeanette shifted in the chair thinking that she could rise and run right now. To the Deetz's house. Tell them everything. Get protection. Have him arrest Brodie.

But Brodie could be pulling down their street right now, and then what?

He'd bust into that house and kill every one of them and not think twice about it.

She couldn't simply pack a bag and drive far away, because he had a bug on her car somewhere which enabled him to see exactly where she was—and follow her. He'd made that clear a million times.

Needing to stand, to stretch, Jeanette arose from the chair, set her knitting aside, and headed for the kitchen. She passed the framed picture on the wall that Brodie insisted they leave up—of them and the kids, Blake and Shelly, when they were still teenagers.

Neither of the kids wanted anything to do with their father now. And who could blame them? Their childhood had been a walking-on-eggshells nightmare of trying to please a domineering, Jekyll-and-Hyde father who could turn on the charm one moment and turn into a cruel and wounding aggressor the next.

Blake and Shelly each called Jeanette several times a year. Brodie allowed the calls, and after each one he would force Jeanette to tell him everything they'd talked about. For some reason Brodie forbid any type of written communication between Jeanette and the kids, such as texts, emails, or letters.

Jeanette went to the fridge, got an apple, and washed it. She dried it and thought about the time several years ago when Blake told her about a magazine article his wife Catherine had written that had been published in a popular Christian magazine. Jeanette found it online. It told, from Catherine's viewpoint, how Blake had followed in Brodie's footsteps, living a married life filled with abuse and terror, fueled by his narcissism and demand for control.

Blake then became a Christian and they were able to salvage their marriage.

Brodie, on the other hand, would never change.

She knew that at the core of her being.

He was a very bad seed, and Jeanette had come to believe that certain people, like him, were made that way and existed to fulfill evil purposes.

She got a paring knife out of the block and sliced the apple in half.

After years of abuse and torment, Jeanette had become so used to the way things were that it was difficult to picture any other way of life. As long as Brodie was a free man, he would own Jeanette. He would not have it any other way. She would never be able to live alone or have another man, because Brodie would hound her to the ends of the earth to be her master.

She cut the apple into thin slices, eating one as she did, and recalled how, twice, she had seriously contemplated suicide.

Outsiders may question why she didn't just run away, or tell someone at the grocery store, or drive to a police or fire station? The answer was simple. Brodie was a sweet talker who had nine lives. He would have gotten out on bail or some other loophole—even for a day—and he would have tracked her down and killed her —in the most excruciating way.

People didn't know.

No one knew what she was going through, or what he was capable of.

She often thought she would never be able to fit into society again because she was so mentally scarred.

"Jeanette, honey."

The spooky voice came from one of the kitchen cameras.

It was him.

Brodie.

"You're bleeding."

Her heart thundered and she froze, staring toward where she thought the voice came from.

"Look down, you simpleton!"

Her head dropped to her chest.

She cursed at the sight of the blood mingled with apple, then felt the burn from the small slice on her left thumb. She examined it, sucked it, crossed to the sink and ran it under water, then wrapped it in a piece of paper towel.

"What on earth, Jeanette?" Brodie barked.

The cut pulsed at the tip of her thumb. "I'm going upstairs to dress it," she said.

"Hold your horses one minute. I'll tell you when you can go. What was that stunt earlier, with Joanie Deetz? The more I think about it the madder I get. Why did you answer the door in the first place? You know the rules."

Jeanette bit her tongue.

She had to be submissive, especially now that the Deetzes were getting so close to blowing the lid off of Brodie's sick world.

If she wasn't submissive, she would pay dearly for it. And the thought of those repercussions gave her a warm, wavy, sick feeling inside that made her need to go to the bathroom.

"Answer me!" he yelled from the tiny speaker.

She squeezed the wet paper towel tighter on her burning thumb, close to tears.

She was so sick of this.

He didn't care about her, about the cut.

He cared about his control over her.

That was all that ever mattered. It was always all about him.

It all just boiled over.

"Do you even care I cut myself?" she yelled, looking at the wall where his voice had come from.

The silence afterward was deafening.

She felt bolder with him not able to reach her.

"Where are you, anyway?" she said.

The wall was silent for some thirty seconds.

She was nervous but felt a freedom she hadn't felt in years.

"What does it matter to you? What's going on, Jeanette?" Brodie paused. "Those Deetzes better not be emboldening you, giving you ideas. Because you know what I'll do. I'll burn it all down, Jeanette. All of it. We'll move again. I don't care. I have no ties here."

"I'm just trying to be nice to the neighbors," she said. "Giving her those eggs was one step toward repairing the damage between us."

He cut her off, yelling. "You're not to answer the door when I'm gone! Period. Now you go dress that cut and go to bed. I'm watching you. And we're going to have a long talk tomorrow about your poor choices today. And about the way you've addressed me this evening. Now, go!"

Jeanette searched the room almost frantically. It wasn't fair. She wanted to lash out. Tell him exactly what kind of a sick, psychopath he was.

But that wouldn't save her.

It would make things worse.

Just do what he says for now.

Stay alive until they catch him.

"Were you about to say something else you're going to regret?" he said.

"No."

She disappeared from his sight, doing as he said.

27

———

IT WAS early Wednesday morning in the quiet Deetz kitchen, three days before Christmas. Joanie—still in her pajamas, robe, and slippers—handed Wayne a plate of scrambled eggs, toast, and banana. "Will you pour us more coffee?" she asked. "And turn the heat up, will you? It's freezing in here."

"Yes, dear," he said in an exaggerated tone, to be funny.

Wayne—dressed warmly for work—filled their cups, went to the hallway and turned the heat up, and met her as they sat down at the kitchen table.

It was another cold, wet day when the damp chill in the air seemed to seep right into the house. It was still dark outside.

"Do you smell smoke?" Wayne said, unfolding his napkin.

Joanie sniffed and unfolded hers. "I don't think so."

Wayne prayed thanks for the food and blessing on their day, and prayed for each of the kids.

"I read that article by the Enoch's daughter-in-law," she said.

"You told me that when I came to bed," he said.

"Oh, did I? Did I tell you they've lived in a lot of different places," she said, referring to the Enochs.

"No. Where? How'd you find that out?"

"Just did a lot of digging around online, social media, putting pieces together. They moved here from Sacramento. And before that, Bakersfield and Carson City, not necessarily in that order."

"I suppose he could work anywhere with his job," Wayne said.

"Wayne, if you could have seen Jeanette yesterday," Joanie said. "She *wants* to tell us. She needs help. Her face and body language are crying out, but she's scared to death of that creep."

He shook his head and wiped his mouth with a napkin. "He's going to make a mistake."

"Isn't there any more we can do right now? Jeanette just doesn't look good, physically."

"All we can do is keep our eyes peeled. From a police standpoint, no."

"What about that recording thingamajig?"

He nodded. "Yeah, that could lead to something. I'll know today. Hopefully they can trace it back to him, but it may be a longshot."

Joanie felt helpless. She was scared for Jeanette. And she was frightened to be living so close to what appeared to be a very deranged man.

"Will you pray?" Joanie said.

"Sure." Wayne took her hand. "Father in heaven, whatever's going on next door, we need you to *expose* it, to shine your floodlights down and help Jeanette. Protect her. Protect *us*. We think of the times in the Bible when evil people hid traps and snares, but the Psalmist said, 'You are my God and strong deliverer. Do not grant the wicked their desires or let their plans succeed.' For Brodie, we pray that his mischief will engulf him, and that burning coals will fall on him. We know bad things are happening in that house. Stop it, Lord. Deliver that house from evil. And put your angels all around Jeanette and us in the meantime."

They said their amens, squeezed hands, and shared a quick kiss.

"There's a campground past where Brodie was headed," Wayne said. "It's called Meander Falls. I'm thinking he may have been heading there. His Jeep's back now. It wasn't when I went to bed last night."

Wayne sniffed again, walked over and opened the back door to the screen porch. He stepped out.

Within a few seconds, Joanie called out to him, "Now I smell it."

He came back in and closed the door. "I don't know how you could burn anything in this weather. It's definitely smoke."

"He probably burned all my underwear out there."

"Mom?" Leena's voice came from around the corner. "I thought you were going to wake me up!" Leena padded into the kitchen in her light robe and fluffy white slippers.

Joanie looked at the clock and said, "You said seven-fifty."

"Seven-fifteen, *fifteen*," Leena said. "I need to be to work at eight."

"What's wrong with your alarm?" Wayne said.

"The volume on the radio is messed up. It goes in and out. It's like from 1980 or something."

"I'm her backup," Joanie said.

"Sounds like you need a new alarm clock," Wayne said. "Look on Amazon. Order one with my credit card and you can pay me for it."

"Dad, honestly?" Leena said. "That should come with my room, it's like part of the house. That's your responsibility to have those household items for those who live here."

Joanie looked at Wayne and they burst out laughing.

"What is so funny?" Leena said. "I'll order one, Dad, but it's on you. Okay?"

"No, no, no, no," Wayne said. "You have more money than you know what to do with."

Leena shrugged. "I'm a saver. What can I say? I've been listening to Dave Ramsey. You'll never catch me in debt, I have an emergency fund, and I'm investing for my future."

"I'll tell you what, I'll split it with you," Wayne said. "How about that?"

"Deal," Leena said.

"Whoa, that was easy," Wayne said reaching out to give her a hug.

"You want breakfast?" Joanie said.

"No, thanks," Leena said. "I'll grab a chicken biscuit there."

"You better get moving," Wayne said.

"I am, I am." Leena said, heading for the stairs. "By the way, I saw old, creepy Brodie get home last night. His coat was torn."

Joanie lost her breath. "What?"

"Right here," Leena reached up and patted the outside of her own bicep. "A square was torn."

"What time was that?" Wayne said.

"I didn't look at my clock, but it had to be after midnight. I heard him pull in."

They all exchanged glances.

"Should we be worried about this wingnut?" Leena said.

"No, honey," Wayne said. "Don't you worry about it."

Joanie gave Leena a hug and told her to hurry up and get ready for work.

Wayne's phone vibrated from his coat pocket. He got it out, looked at the screen, told Joanie it was Googan, and answered. "This is Deetz."

"Googan here. You got a minute?"

"Sure. I'm on my way in . . ."

"I just wanted to tell you; I got a text late last night from the male dancer at that club where Dawn danced."

Deetz waited.

"Our person of interest showed up like an hour before closing," Googan said. "I got there as fast as I could, but he was gone."

"Was anyone with him?" Deetz asked.

"Negative. The bartender at the time—who's also a female dancer there—said he sat at the bar for half-an-hour, trying to cozy up to her, but she wasn't having it. She also told me he asked where Dawn Delight was. The bartender didn't know anything about this guy—our person of interest—but now she does, and she'll call me if he shows up again."

"Hmm. Wow. Anything else?"

"Other than the fact that he had a bandage on his forehead, no. The male dancer who texted me was hoping to get a license plate or take a picture of the guy, but he was dancing almost the whole time our guy was there. He just shot me off a text; that was the best he could do."

"Good work, Googan. Thanks for going the extra mile last night."

"Like I told you, these type cases are what I'm all about."

"All right. Good. I'm on my way in. You?"

"I'll see you there. I've found a couple cold cases I want to delve into. Other missing dancers. I'll keep you posted."

28

———————

ROXANNE GREW MORE nervous by the second as Randall pulled
her car into the driveway at the Deetz house, with her in the
passenger seat. It was close to noon on Wednesday. She took one
last giant hit from her vape pen and blew a huge cloud of smoke out
the cracked car window; half of it blew back in.

"You better not do that while you're here," Randall said, stopping the car and turning it off. "These people are not going to want
to be smelling strawberry shortcake for the next week."

"Oh, stop." She fumbled around with trembling hands to open
her purse and tossed the pen inside. "I don't know why I'm so
nervous. Come with me, will you? Bring my bag?"

"After how I acted at the wedding?" he said. "Don't make me do
that. Just relax. You're going to be fine. These are good people."

"Please, Randall, look at this weather. Just get me to the door."

He huffed and shook his head and opened his door.

Roxanne opened her door to get out. "Barging in here during
Christmas. I'm thinking this was a bad idea."

Randall shut his door and popped the trunk. She waited for him,
pulling her hood over her head in the windy rain. He hoisted the
large tan suitcase out of the back with a grunt. "Holy cow, Roxanne,
what's in here, dumbbells?"

"Hand me the smaller bag, please," she said, waving a hand
at it.

147

He got that one out and his jaw dropped open. "I honestly want to know what's in these bags."

"Shut up. I had to bring gifts. Plus, my hair dryer and all the accessories."

She reached for the smaller bag, but Randall threw it over his shoulder and wheeled the suitcase. "Come on. Let's get out of this rain."

They got up to the door at the front porch and before Roxanne rang the doorbell, the door opened, and Joanie Deetz welcomed them inside. The house was warm and cozy, with ivy and white Christmas lights on the stair rail and a hand-carved manger scene prominently displayed there in the foyer. The way Joanie hugged Roxanne and warmly shook Randall's hand, smiled, and greeted him so congenially immediately set Roxanne more at ease.

Randall had humbly said goodbye and turned to leave but then looked back at Joanie. "Uh, Mrs. Deetz?" he said.

Joanie turned back and opened her eyes wide as if to say, "Yes?"

"I want to tell you how sorry I am about the scene I made at the wedding and the reception." He looked Joanie right in the eyes and Roxanne was touched by his genuineness. "I have no excuses. I'd had too much to drink, which is never good, and I had a big chip on my shoulder. You and Wayne have been more than gracious." He nodded shyly. "Anyway, I hope I can make it up to you somehow."

Joanie, of course, shooed him off as if it had been nothing, but Roxanne knew their behavior that evening had been abhorrent. The Deetzes truly were gracious people.

As Randall was leaving, Joanie said, "I'm praying for you this week, that all goes well and that you two will be able to reunite soon."

"Thank you very much." Randall nodded and barged out into the weather.

Joanie acted as if Roxanne was part of the family. She showed her to her bedroom upstairs, which used to have been Brandon's room. It had its own miniature manger scene and a small tabletop Christmas tree with tiny lights and decorations. She showed her what would be her own bathroom with fresh towels and washcloths and pointed out Leena's room along the way. Next, she gave

Roxanne a tour of the house, showing her different comfy places where she could be alone to read or whatever.

As they got to the kitchen, Joanie said, "Now, I have some lunch ready for us. It's nothing fancy, just some chicken salad sandwiches, chips, and veggies." The table had already been set for two and Joanie moved with grace as she retrieved the croissant sandwiches from the fridge, put some chips into a wood bowl, and fixed glasses of ice water for each of them.

"You are too kind to be doing this for me—for us—especially right at Christmas," Roxanne said. "Thank you so much. It's an embarrassing situation."

"We're family now, right?" Joanie said. "It will be fun to have you here—with Kristen and Brandon. We usually all go to Christmas Eve service together."

"Oh, that will be lovely," Roxanne said, wondering if Randall would also be invited—and whether he would come or not, if he was.

Joanie closed her eyes briefly before starting. Roxanne assumed she'd said a blessing.

"Oh, I forgot," Joanie stood, "I've got some pickles to go with this." She went to the fridge.

Meanwhile, her phone buzzed between their places at the kitchen table.

Roxanne couldn't help but look at the screen.

It was a text message—from Wayne Deetz:

> They are trying to trace the listening device
> right now!

29

———

IT WAS EARLY AFTERNOON, and Jeanette still couldn't shake the fog from her head. She held the ice bag to her left temple, which was swollen and tender from where Brodie had punched her in the middle of the night—part of her punishment for answering the door that day when Joanie Deetz had come over. Actually, Jeanette was surprised Brodie's discipline hadn't been worse. Fortunately, he had been preoccupied with other more pressing concerns.

She kept her eyes glued to the stairs in case he would come down from his office. She could *not* let him see the ice pack. The one and only time she had ever used one after one of his beatings, he'd gone ballistic; the ice pack had reminded him of the maniacal damage he'd inflicted. When he hurt her, he wanted no reminders. He wanted to completely erase it from his memory; believe he wasn't the monster he really was.

Jeanette wondered if the woman, Dawn, was still alive.

Probably not.

As she stared at the steps in a daze, awaiting Brodie's next move, she drifted back to the early morning hours when he had returned home. It was about 2 a.m. The upper arm of his coat had been torn and there was a bandage on his forehead. Jeanette could only guess that Dawn had put up a fight.

Poor woman.

Brodie had barged in, turned on all the lights, and dragged

Jeanette from the bed. She'd been awake anyway, of course, dreading his return. He'd ranted and raved and paced, smacking her once, hard, for opening the door to Joanie. But he'd seemed more concerned with the interference of Wayne Deetz whom, he complained venomously, had followed him that afternoon when he'd left in the camper van.

Had Brodie hurt Deetz? Was that why he had paced around like a caged animal?

Or was he nervous because he sensed Deetz was closing in on him?

That rare glimmer of hope had made her heart soar and almost took her breath away.

Jeanette had been so curious she'd dared to ask Brodie what had happened when Deetz followed him, but Brodie refused to address it with her.

She knew him. He was calculating something, planning his next steps. This had happened before. And each time he got like this they had pulled up stakes and moved.

"I've got to take care of something out back," Brodie had said in the night. "I need you to turn out the lights and keep an eye on the front of the house." He'd dug her phone out of his pocket and jabbed it into her hands. "Any sign of cops or firetrucks or anything else, you call my phone. I'll be in the backyard. Understand?"

At two in the morning?

She'd nodded that she understood as he began stripping off his clothes.

"I said, 'Do you understand?'" he'd yelled.

"Yes. I understand, Brodie." She turned out most of the lights in the house and went to one of the front bedrooms that looked down on the quiet street. Nothing was moving out there. She sat on the corner of the bed in silence.

She wondered if Brodie was going to bury something in the backyard—or someone.

Her temple pounded where he'd hit her, and she felt it swelling. She stared out the window in a daze of dejection and sleeplessness.

Within minutes she snapped to her senses when she caught a whiff of smoke.

Her heart had instantly begun banging against her ribcage, thinking he may be burning down the house—with her in it.

She checked the street once more—all quiet—and hurried back into their bedroom at the back of the house and peered out the window down into the backyard.

Flames danced in front of Brodie's silhouette at the fire pit he'd once dug for burning leaves, debris, and downed branches.

She could clearly see the jeans and coat he'd been wearing minutes ago, now smoking and catching fire.

He squeezed a bottle of lighter fluid, the clear liquid arched toward the blaze, and the flames jumped higher. He repeated the process until he had a bonfire, the smoke and ash churning up through the trees and into the night sky.

She'd never seen him do this.

There was a thick, misty rain in the air but that wasn't going to stop him.

He wore only sweatpants, a T-shirt, and Crocs.

His head twitched as he stood over the fire.

A large bag sat next to him on the ground. He squeezed more lighter fluid onto the blaze, set the bottle down, and threw the whole bag onto the fire. It smoldered for some time. He picked up what looked like a five-foot walking stick and jabbed at the items in the blaze until they finally burst into flames.

Brodie had poked and poked and poked, making sure everything caught fire.

It had all been so surreal.

This was her life now.

She knew marriage—life—wasn't supposed to be this way, she knew that, but she didn't know any other way.

Whose things were in that bag that he burned? Joanie's? Dawn's? Mine? Someone else's?

She recalled how, as if sensing her thoughts, Brodie had suddenly turned and looked up at the window where she stood in the shadows in the night.

She'd slowly leaned away.

The room had been black so he couldn't see her. But it felt like he could.

His "look" had jarred her out of her daze, and she'd hurried back to check the front of the house.

Unfortunately, everything had been just as quiet as before.

And now, here she was some twelve hours later, icepack on her temple, staring at the steps, waiting on eggshells for Brodie's next move.

What a way to live.

She heard nothing. He was still buried in his office.

It was early afternoon, three days before Christmas. She adjusted the icepack at her temple and squinted as she took a glance at the backyard. It was a bright, gray, cold day. Very damp.

The burning pit wasn't smoldering anymore. Brodie had been out there earlier that morning, watering the area down with a hose and covering it with leaves, sticks, and debris from the woods.

There was no sign of the fire, except for the lingering smell of smoke and ash.

30

D EETZ PACED the shiny concrete floor in the basement hallway at Portland Police Bureau headquarters, just outside the doors of the Digital Analysis & Response Unit. The tiny device Joanie had found under their bed was being examined and, hopefully, traced by a high-IQ digital specialist named Barry Lanier. But it had been hours and Deetz was beginning to have his doubts whether the young man could pull it off.

If indeed they could trace the device to Brodie Enoch, Deetz's plan was to arrest him for eavesdropping using a recording device. Deetz knew it was a crime, and when he researched the specifics he found that it was illegal in Portland to obtain the contents of a conversation using any device without the informed consent of all participants. Although violating the law was only a Class A misdemeanor—which could carry a penalty of up to a year in jail and a fine—Deetz was convinced that once he had Brodie in custody, the man's house of cards would fall. Jeanette would talk and they could nail Brodie for domestic violence, the home break in, and who knew what else?

Deetz strode into the doorless breakroom and examined the contents of side-by-side vending machines. Nothing looked good. Of course, Googan was late. They'd agreed to meet there at two but there was no sign of him. Deetz's phone buzzed. It was a text from Joanie:

Randall dropped Roxanne so she's here. He
apologized for his behavior at the wedding. We
girls had a nice lunch. All will be well. Any more on
the device? Love you.

The text reminded Deetz that he still needed to call Randall and share the good news about his major coup that morning. He glanced up and down the hallway and didn't see Googan yet, so he dialed Randall.

"Hello Wayne," Randall answered.

"Randall, I have some good news," Deetz said.

"Well, that I could use."

"I was finally able to track down the woman who hired those bad boys to pay you the visit at Roxanne's house."

"Oh?"

"Yeah. It turns out she's no angel herself," Deetz said. "You've heard the expression, 'It takes one to know one?' Well, that kind lady was found guilty of poisoning and killing her neighbor's dogs —two of them. She got off with a fine, community service, and psychological counseling."

"Holy cow. You don't say."

"That's not all. She had a long-time dispute with another neighbor about property boundaries and ended up hiring someone to run the wife off the road. She did a year-and-a-half for that at Columbia River Correctional."

"No way."

"It's true. I just couldn't picture a poor, old broken-down widow hiring those thugs to work you over, so I did some digging."

"I'll be. Thank you, Wayne."

"I let her know that we could and would arrest her and charge her with attempted murder and conspiracy to commit murder if she didn't call those goons off—so I'm hoping you're in the clear. Of course, Roxanne can stay with us as long as you want, until we know the coast is clear. I've not told her or Joanie yet. I wanted to call you first."

The phone was silent.

Deetz thought the connection had dropped.

"Randall?" he said.

"I . . . I don't know what to say to you."

"Well, she of course went into detail about the fraud she says you committed against her, but—"

"But it's true."

"But it didn't hold up in court. God's giving you a break, man. He wants that new start for you. At least that's what it looks like from here."

Randall cleared his throat. "I want that, more than anything. But I owe that lady."

"Well, pay her back if you want. I know you said it's a lot of money, but still, you could save up and pay her what you can. You could do it anonymously. I don't know. I'm not sure that's the right move. Maybe you just got a clean break."

"I was able to pay one lady back. It was a recent thing. I don't think she even had time to know it had happened. I wish I could pay them all back."

After another moment of silence, Randall said, "Why are you doing this? Especially after the way I acted at the wedding?"

"Ha. Well, I was just reading this morning that we're forgiven by the same measure that we forgive others—so I need to be pretty forgiving." Deetz chuckled at himself. "Have you heard the story of the Good Samaritan?"

"I've heard the term Good Samaritan, but that's about it," Randall said.

"Well, read it sometime. You're the guy who's been beaten and is lying on the side of the road. He needs a helping hand. Although others may not want to help you for whatever reason, I feel called to help you—to help get you that new start."

Randall sniffed and Deetz realized he may be crying.

"I promise you I'm going to make the most of it," Randall said.

Harry Googan ambled into the breakroom out of breath. He gave Deetz a quick wave and hoisted his bulging backpack onto one of the black metal tables. While he sat down and pulled out a crumpled legal pad and got his laptop fired up, Deetz ended the call with Randall, then approached the big man.

"Late, as usual," Deetz said, resigned to the fact the guy would always be late. What did Deetz care at this point? He had exactly nine days left until he was done with this gig, and that didn't take into account a day off for Christmas and another for New Year's Eve.

"Yeah, and you're going to be glad to know why," Googan said, taking an enormous bite of a fast-food hamburger that appeared out of nowhere.

"Tell me," Deetz said.

With a mouthful, Googan said, "I found . . . cold case . . . California . . . like Dawn . . ."

"Go ahead and swallow," Deetz urged him. "I can't understand you."

Googan grimaced and frowned with food on his front teeth and forced the burger down as if he was swallowing a mouse. He put a fist to his chest and belched silently.

"Sorry about that," Googan said. "Okay, I'll start from the past and work my way to present. I found a cold case in Bakersfield, California, very similar to Dawn Delight. Club dancer. Early thirties. Disappeared late one weeknight, near closing time. Same thing. She was waiting for a Lyft driver. That was in 2018."

Bakersfield.

Deetz realized he'd forgotten to text Joanie back. He decided when he got done with Googan he would go check with the digital specialist, then shoot her an update.

"That's just the beginning," Googan said. "Are you listening? You look like you're somewhere else."

"Yeah, yeah. Go ahead."

"I mean, I know you're retiring in a week, but this is some serious stuff. I think we may have a serial killer on our hands. Dawn Delight could be one of many."

That got Deetz's attention.

"Similar case in Reno in 2020," Googan continued, "except this woman—Brianna White, thirty-three years of age—drove an Uber as one of her jobs. She was also a bartender. She went missing after work at the bar. Two-fifteen in the morning. Taken. Her car was found still parked in the parking lot. No cameras. Cold case."

"Not a dancer, though," Deetz said.

"I'm not even close to being finished." Googan rifled through several pages of his notepad. "Here's, another. Christina Brook, thirty-five years young, white." Googan looked up at Deetz. "Keep in mind, they're all white and in their thirties, good looking gals, and all from our region, up and down the West Coast." He looked back down at the pad. "Christina went missing in the early hours of the morning after finishing her shift at a jazz lounge in Carson City, which, as you may or may not know, is close to Reno."

Carson City.

"Was *she* a dancer?"

"It's not clear. The owner makes it out to be a real high-end, hoity-toity club, but from some drilling down I did online, I sense there are some shenanigans going on there—dancing, possibly prostitution."

Something was trying to align in Deetz's head, but it just floated out there with the other million things churning around in his mind.

"When was the jazz club girl taken?"

"That's what I'm talking about!" Googan said. "Reno was 2020. Carson City was 2021. Look at this." Googan whipped through more pages of his notes and pounded his finger on a map of the U.S. that he'd sketched very roughly in pen—it looked like a big blob that a child had drawn. "Bakersfield was the first in 2018. That's southern California. Then he moves north all the way up to Reno and Carson City in 2020 and 2021 . . ."

Deetz watched as Googan pounded each city he'd written on the map.

"He's working his way up to you—to Portland," Googan said. "But he made one more move before that." Googan tapped his finger repeatedly to the left, west, where he'd spelled out Elk Grove in large black ink and something else just above that in smaller letters.

"Elk Grove, California, *was* another dancer. Ellie Workman. Thirty-three. White. And this was in 2023. The owner told me some dude watched her for two or three months and once she disappeared, so did he. I sent the owner the artist's rendering of our guy, and he said, 'That's him.' And he also said the guy had a strange—"

"Investigator Deetz!" Digital specialist Barry Lanier came running into the breakroom. His hands were clasped in front of him. He saw Deetz and hurried over. The young man knew how important that recording device was to Deetz.

"Investigator Deetz. We've got it!" The young man anxiously apologized and excused himself before Googan, fidgeted with his fingers, and then swept his curly black hair back with both hands. He took a deep breath, then exhaled slowly, forcing himself to calm down. He spoke slowly and intentionally. "We were able to trace the phone number of the listening device. It is connected to a burner phone. I should have a name for you in less than ten minutes. You can come with me if you want."

"Yes, okay. Fantastic." Deetz's mind raced. He started to follow Barry Lanier.

"Wait, Deetz. Will you let me finish?" Googan said in a frustrated tone. "It'll only take a minute and you'll be up to speed. There's no need to split this into two meetings. I've got work to do."

He's right.

Deetz shook off his desire to follow the kid. "Go ahead, Barry." He waved. "I've got to finish this up. I'll be there in five minutes."

"You got it, sir." Barry nodded repeatedly and trotted out of the room.

Deetz forced himself to refocus. "Sorry. That's about the break-in at our house," Deetz said to Googan. "Yeah, go ahead, finish telling me."

"No, we're good," Googan said. "The only other thing I was going to say was that the owner of the club in Elk Grove said that the dude who was creeping on Ellie Workman had a very distinct—"

Googan's words faded out and all Deetz could think about was Elk Grove.

Elk Grove, Elk Grove, Elk Grove.

Isn't that near . . .

Deetz's heart thundered.

He zeroed his focus in on the map Googan had drawn.

He put a finger on the map at the big black letters that spelled Elk Grove.

Then he leaned in and looked closer, moving his finger just

above Elk Grove to the other word written smaller, just above it: *Sacramento.*

Everything aligned.

Like two tectonic plates locking together with a loud clang.

Joanie had said the Enochs had lived in all those places, lastly Sacramento.

"Are you listening to me?" Googan shoved his chair back with a loud screech and got to his feet. "I guess we're done here because you're zoned out."

"No, no, I'm not," Deetz said. "I think I know who the killer is."

"What?" Googan's large head craned back. "How could you possibly know?"

"You were about to say he has a tic, weren't you."

Googan's mouth dropped open, and he froze.

"He's my neighbor."

31

JEANETTE WAS BACK in her safe chair, watching out the window as the gray clouds rolled quickly past and the backyard shifted from shady to sunny every few seconds. She decided she'd taken enough chance with the icepack and, besides, the ice had melted. She stood, went to the kitchen, and returned it to the freezer.

On the way, she'd caught a reflection of herself in a mirror in the hallway. She'd lost so much weight, more than twenty pounds since she'd married Brodie. She hated the way she looked. Thin. Pale. Frail is the word that came to mind; that's what he'd made her.

Of all the places they'd lived, she'd never felt closer to possibly getting away—to finding freedom—than right now. Wayne Deetz was no fool, and neither was his wife. They knew something very wrong was happening in the house next door. And Jeanette believed they'd caught glimpses of her wrecked emotional state, her fear and trepidation.

She crossed to the sink, looked out the window, and listened. Not a sound came from Brodie's office upstairs. She often thought, if she ever escaped, what people would say, what they would ask her. "Why didn't you just run? You had a car. He let you go places. Why didn't you just go to the police?"

Fear.

Terror!

If Jeanette did go to the authorities, told all she knew, Brodie would have killed her. Brodie would survive. He'd land on his feet. He always did. He would always be there. He was the kind of person who would have gotten out of anything they questioned him for or even arrested him for. Even if he went to prison, he would either have her murdered while he was in there, or he would wait until he got out and do it himself. He'd told her that, promised it, sworn it. And that promise had so alarmed her that it had made her a captive. She believed she could never escape his clutches—*until now.*

Now, she was feeling something deep inside.

The Deetzes were giving her hope.

Jeanette didn't know for certain what Brodie ultimately did with the women he'd kidnapped and abused. He never talked about it. And she didn't dare ask. But she assumed he killed them, which she couldn't even believe she was thinking. *Her own husband, a cold-blooded killer.* And, by the looks of the scratch on his face and tear in his jacket, he'd probably killed Dawn Delight.

Jeanette quietly headed for the laundry room. There was a load in the dryer she needed to fold. And then she might take a nap. She was finding herself lying down to sleep several times a day now and she knew it was because she was chronically depressed. Naturally she was depressed! Who wouldn't be? Brodie told her she was getting lazy and that she was too skinny. He called her a zombie just a few days ago. Compared to the beautiful women he brought back there, those he'd kidnapped, Jeanette felt like a peasant slave girl.

She shoved the white plastic laundry basket in front of the dryer and removed the clothes that had been sitting in there for some time.

She heard something and stopped what she was doing . . .

From upstairs, Brodie cussed a blue streak at the top of his lungs.

Jeanette couldn't move.

Chills engulfed her and she froze in dread.

The house fell silent.

She stood so still . . . she just wanted to vaporize into nothing. To disappear.

Look at you.

Think about this.

It's all so wrong.

Brodie's office door crashed open.

His footsteps thundered across the hallway upstairs and he flew down the staircase almost without hitting a step.

"Where are you?" he yelled.

What felt like a jolt of electricity zapped her entire being and carved out her insides.

"Laundry room," she called with a trembling voice.

In two seconds, there he was, in her face. His brown eyes were almost black now and they were dancing and frazzled. He took a deep breath and tried to calm himself.

"Pack a suitcase," he tried to level his tone. "We need to get out of here A-S-A-P."

No!

We can't leave now.

The Deetzes are too close!

"Why?" she uttered. "What's happened?"

"I'm being traced, tracked." His narrow ghoulish head flinched uncontrollably several times. She'd come to despise that stone face and those idiotic tics. "It's happening right now, real time. I can see it on my computer. Take clothes, toiletries, essentials. We leave in five minutes."

She had to stall this.

"Traced?" she said. "I don't understand—"

SLAP.

She hadn't seen his backhand coming. Her cheek stung.

"No. More. Questions!" he screamed. "Just do what I say—now! We've got to get out of here."

She was rattled like a puppet on strings for several seconds, then she got her bearings and took off for the stairs.

"Hurry up!" he yelled.

WHILE JEANETTE PACKED as many clothes as she could into her large suitcase, Brodie was frantically running up and down the stairs, hauling the computers from his office down to the garage. By the time he showed up in the bedroom lugging his big suitcase onto the bed, she was in the bathroom filling her toiletry kit.

"Which car are we taking?" Jeanette said.

"Mine," Brodie answered as he stuffed clothes from his drawers into his suitcase.

"Mine's bigger," she said.

"We're taking the Jeep," he blurted.

Oh, that's right, you don't want to leave behind the vehicle that contains the DNA of every poor woman you've taken.

"Where are we going?" she dared ask.

He ignored her as he rushed past her into the closet to pluck some shirts and pants off their hangers.

She peered around the corner at his suitcase and noticed he'd taken the framed family portrait off the wall and packed it.

He lived in a dream world. Did he really think they were a family? The kids despised him.

He hurried by her again and stuffed the clothes from the closet into his suitcase, zipped it closed, and took a deep breath.

"Take your stuff to the Jeep, we're rolling," he said, scanning the room for any last items to throw in.

"Okay," she said, just as an idea came to her like a lightning bolt.

Leave a note for the Deetzes. A trail.

"Where are we going?" she asked again, as gently as possible.

Standing there face-to-face, with their suitcases between them, ready to go, his mouth sealed into a slit, his head tilted, and he raised a fist and whispered, "If you ask me that one more time, so help me . . ."

32

———

Joanie didn't send Christmas cards anymore because it had begun to feel like a rote obligation; she'd stopped probably three or four years ago. But she'd recently received a heartfelt card from an old high school classmate, so she'd decided to send her a letter. The whole time Joanie had written it and then addressed and stamped the envelope at the kitchen table, pausing now and then to stare out the window, she'd heard Roxanne talking on the phone in the den—although she wasn't able to understand any of it.

Now, Roxanne appeared in the doorway with her arms crossed. "Well, that husband of yours is really something," she said with a huge smile.

"What's he done now?" Joanie said, getting up from the table.

"That was Randall. He had some very good news." Roxanne explained how Wayne had managed to track down the woman who'd paid to have Randall worked over. Wayne had apparently threatened her with some serious 'criminal' consequences if she didn't call off her goon squad. "I mean, I might not even need to be in your hair for Christmas," Roxanne said. "Although Randall did say Wayne thinks I should stay through the deadline they gave him, just to be sure."

"Well, that *is* good news," Joanie said.

"I can't believe it. I've been worried sick. This is like a whole new beginning."

"I'm so happy for you."

"You and Wayne, your family, you've been so good to us," Roxanne said. "Even after the fiasco at the wedding . . . our behavior."

Joanie closed her eyes, smiled, and touched Roxanne's clasped hands. "I'm glad things are working out for you. We're going to make it a festive Christmas." She held up the envelope. "I'm going to put this out for the mail lady, although I probably missed her. Help yourself to anything. I want you to make yourself at home and treat this like a little vacation."

Roxanne laughed. "I'll do that. In fact, I think I'll take a little cat nap in my room in a few minutes."

"Sounds like a lovely idea. There are extra blankets in your closet."

Joanie threw on a light blue hoodie from the hallway closet and headed out the front door. She took the sidewalk and began walking down the driveway, thinking how good it was to see and feel the sun. Christmas was indeed going to be interesting. They would invite Randall for Christmas dinner on Saturday, which Joanie planned to serve around 2 p.m. She counted the guests again— nine, including their family of five, plus Roxanne, Randall, Tammy, and Kristen. She went over the menu again in her mind: spiral sliced ham, the potato casserole the kids loved, cold veggie salad, cheap white rolls, and Kristen and Tammy were bringing desserts. She wondered if Roxanne would want to go to the candlelight service on Christmas Eve with them; perhaps they'd invite Randall, too. They usually got Chinese take-out on Christmas Eve before the service, but she hadn't had a chance to talk to Wayne about what they wanted to do yet.

Joanie heard something next door.

Without looking, she realized it was Brodie's low, stern voice.

The hair on the back of her neck stood straight up.

The thought of him sickened her.

She still didn't look, but approached the mailbox, then turned around and took a quick glance as she bent over and opened the door of the mailbox.

Brodie and Jeanette stood at the back of his Jeep. Her arms were crossed and she looked as bashful as ever. Just before he closed the back door Joanie noticed the Jeep was packed to the gills with suit-cases, computer equipment, and plastic bags. He slammed the back door but couldn't get it closed. He tried two more times, cursing each time until it shut.

He's hot about something.

Jeanette got in the passenger side and Brodie headed for the driver's door.

Good, maybe they're spending Christmas away.

Joanie looked into the mailbox.

Darn.

The mail lady had come already.

Oh well.

She took the four or five pieces of mail from the box, put her letter in, closed the door, and flipped up the red metal flag.

Then she stopped cold.

Brodie was staring at her with one hand on the car door handle.

A rush of fright hit Joanie like a wave of prickly heat.

Suddenly, Brodie threw the door open, jumped in, slammed the door, and the Jeep revved to life.

As Brodie stood just outside the Jeep staring at the street, Jeanette turned around in the passenger seat to see what he was looking at.

It was Joanie Deetz, at her mailbox.

Oh, no.

Jeanette's heart began to beat faster.

Should she put her window down and yell to Joanie when they backed up? Scream for help?

After all, they were never coming back there. This would be the last time she ever saw this house.

It would make Brodie furious, but it may be Jeanette's last chance to cry for help. At least Joanie would hear it and know for certain Jeanette was in trouble and the authorities needed to pursue.

The driver's door ripped open and Brodie jumped in and started the Jeep.

"We're taking Joanie Deetz with us." He glanced at Jeanette and jammed it into Reverse.

It took a second for his words to register.

"What?" Jeanette murmured. "There's . . . there's no room."

He goosed the Jeep backward.

"You *make* room," he ordered.

Jeanette looked back and Joanie had started walking back up the driveway toward her house.

"No, Brodie, please. Not Joanie. Don't! Please."

Brodie ignored her and the Jeep vaulted backward toward Joanie Deetz.

33

Roxanne responded to several text messages in the den, gathered a few things, and headed for the stairs. She knew she was going to sleep like a baby. She was so relieved about Randall. Maybe she would shoot him a text before her nap and tell him how excited she was about their future.

A phone rang in the kitchen, probably Joanie's.

Roxanne had gone up two steps, but curiosity got the best of her. She went to the kitchen, spotted Joanie's phone on the table, and went over and took a look. Wayne was calling.

Roxanne ignored it and headed back toward the staircase.

Ding.

Now a text message on Joanie's phone.

Roxanne turned around, walked past the phone into the front room and looked out the window to see where Joanie was—still walking back from the mailbox.

Roxanne crossed back to Joanie's phone. The screen had gone black. She picked it up and the text lit up—it was from Wayne:

> Brodie's a killer. Get out now. Go anywhere. Go to
> Leena's work. Take Roxanne. Now! We're coming
> for him.

Roxanne's head craned back. She squinted at the phone and

read the message again with alarm. She set her shoulders back and her eyes darted about the house, the wheels in her head spun.

Joanie's phone rang again.

She looked at it.

Wayne Deetz, again. *He's desperate to reach Joanie.*

Roxanne's mind reeled. *A killer? Could this have anything to do with Randall?*

She answered the call. "Wayne? It's Roxanne." She walked toward the front window. "Joanie's getting the mail, but I saw your text . . ."

"Roxanne, you and Joanie need to get out of there, *now*. The man next door is a killer—"

"Next door?" She looked out the window at Joanie, carrying some mail as she walked.

A Jeep was backing up in the driveway next door.

"Yes, Brodie Enoch. Next door," Wayne said. "You two need to leave, just to be safe. We're on our way, but I want you guys away from there. Leena's at work, correct?"

"Ah, yes . . ."

Without warning, the Jeep swerved and rocketed right through the lawn toward Joanie.

"Oh, dear Lord!" Roxanne screamed.

She dropped the phone and ran for the front door, thinking she needed a weapon of some kind. Anything. She stopped and scanned the foyer and what she could see of the downstairs.

Deetz was yelling into the discarded phone.

Roxanne had no time to waste.

There!

She ran to a bookshelf in the family room and grabbed a brass bookend in the shape of an eagle's head. It was heavy. Books spilled onto the floor. Her heart thundered in her chest as she ran for the front door.

34

———————

Joanie stopped in shock.

The Jeep barreled toward her in Reverse. Right through the grass!

She dropped the mail and darted left, through the lawn, toward the house.

The Jeep swerved in her direction, banged over the blacktop driveway, and into the grass again continuing directly toward her.

Roxanne came running down the front steps carrying something.

Within only fifteen feet of Joanie the Jeep tried to stop abruptly but skidded and fishtailed like a whip through the wet grass, then came to a halt with steam billowing up from the tires.

Joanie heard herself scream thinking he was coming to get her.

Sure enough, the driver's door banged open, and Brodie Enoch jumped out and raced toward her like some soldier on a mission.

Roxanne was hurrying toward her through the grass.

"Stop!" Roxanne yelled.

Joanie began to run toward the front door of the house, but it was still forty feet away. She had to get in and lock the door. She had to get Roxanne back in, too.

"Roxanne, come with me," she yelled.

She could feel Brodie catching up to her. Could almost feel his breath.

Roxanne was coming toward her.

"Get away!" Roxanne screamed at Brodie.

Joanie caught a glimpse of Jeanette, standing by the Jeep, arms crossed, chewing her cuticles.

Roxanne dashed between Joanie and Brodie.

Joanie stopped and turned to face them; she couldn't let Roxanne get hurt.

Roxanne lifted what Joanie could see now was one of the brass bookends over her right shoulder and hurled it toward Brodie with a grunt.

His eyes grew large, and he blocked the object with a wrist, cussing when it hit him.

For a split-second, everyone stopped, like someone hit pause in a movie.

Then Brodie darted for Roxanne, grabbed her at the top of her arms, and threw her rolling and sprawling onto the ground. The only noise Roxanne made was a ghastly grunt when she hit the ground.

Then he came at Joanie.

She turned and ran for the house, but he tackled her before she'd gone three steps.

She rolled over kicking, squirming, and fighting.

"You're coming with me," he said forcefully through clenched jaw, fighting off her kicks and scratches with a sick laugh.

No.

I cannot get in that Jeep.

"Stop it!" Roxanne yelled.

Still on her back, Joanie kicked furiously, ripped her arms away, and writhed back and forth to avoid his grasp.

"Oh . . . you are a wild cat," Brodie said out of breath, hair in his eyes. "I like that."

Color and motion from the left.

Roxanne with the bookend above her head.

She cried out as she bashed his skull with a sick thud.

Brodie's grip instantly released.

His eyes rolled.

Without a word he collapsed onto Joanie.

She screamed disgustedly and scrambled out from beneath him.

The back of his head was bleeding.

Roxanne stood bent over them, her hands on her knees, gasping for air.

Joanie got to her knees and slowly to her feet.

Over next to the Jeep, Jeanette was on her knees in the grass, her head in her hands on the ground, her shoulders lurching, crying tears of freedom.

35

———

Deetz, Googan, Tidwell, and two Portland police officers arrived in two cars with sirens blaring just as Brodie Enoch came to.

Googan cuffed him roughly and read him his rights as Joanie explained what had happened with a trembling voice. Deetz was so furious he felt like strangling Brodie, but the man's head was swollen and he was still groggy.

"Roxanne was unbelievable," Joanie said with her arms crossed and shivering from the shock. "Thank God she was here. I just . . . I still can't believe it. He would have had me. Do you hear me, Wayne. I'd be gone."

Brodie sneered at her. His forehead was drenched in sweat and his hair was matted with blood.

Deetz put his arms around Roxanne and Joanie and hugged them both. "Thank God," he whispered. "Thank you, Roxanne."

She just whimpered and nodded. "Wait till Randall hears about this."

Tidwell talked one-on-one with Jeanette, still over by the Jeep, standing there with her hands in the prayer position against her mouth. She had not wanted to go near Brodie and did not even look his way.

"We know you kidnapped Regina Hart—a.k.a. Dawn Delight— from the Pole Barn," Googan said to Brodie. "Where is she? Is she still alive?"

Brodie was still breathing hard. His mouth twitched and he smiled. Then he said in the calmest of voices, "I have no idea *who* that is or *what* you're talking about. I'm one hundred percent innocent and I want my lawyer involved *now.*"

"Just like you don't know anything about the others?" Googan said. "Bakersfield. Carson City. Sacramento. You like them in their thirties. Dancers."

Brodie's face contorted in defense. "You're nuts, man. You've got nothing on me."

"No?" Deetz said. "We traced the recording device to you, that you put in our bedroom. You did that when you robbed our house."

"And I'm sure we'll find plenty more when forensics does the once-over on your Jeep and that camper van," Googan said.

"Where is the camper van?" Deetz said. "Meander Falls? Is that where you were headed when I was following you? Is that where Regina is?"

Brodie laughed. "Yeah, what happened to you that day, anyway? You were following me, then you weren't. You must've gotten side-tracked."

Deetz's face flushed.

He looked over at Jeanette and Tidwell. He had her talking and was taking notes on a small pad.

Good.

Lord, let her tell it all.

"What're you lookin' at Deetz?" Brodie said, nodding toward Jeanette. "She's not gonna talk, you know. Never. You're barking up the wrong tree with her."

"What'd you do, Brodie, threaten to kill her?" Deetz said. "Threaten you'd track her down and cut her into pieces if she talked? That sounds like you, mister happy-go-lucky serial killer."

Brodie jerked his handcuffed wrists and scowled at Deetz, his shoulders flinching. Then he shook his head and chuckled. "You know what's so funny about all this? We were good neighbors to you. Stopped in to visit. Brought you gifts." Brodie blinked repeatedly. "And what do we get in return? You search our home. And now this?" Brodie's face darkened and he frowned. "I have a feeling you're going to pay for the way you've treated us."

Deetz stepped toward him, leaned in close to Brodie's face, and whispered. "You moved into the wrong house, Brodie. You picked on the wrong people."

Brodie seethed.

Deetz continued. "My advice to you is, take a good look around at the trees and the sky. Breathe in this fresh Oregon air. Because this is the last of it for you. Now, you're going to know what your wife has known all these years—what it feels like to be behind bars."

Brodie lunged at Deetz, but Googan, who already had him by the bicep, ripped him backward, almost throwing him to the ground.

Deetz looked over toward Jeanette, and Tidwell waved him over.

The grass was still wet, and the Jeep had left thick mud tracks where it had skidded.

"There's a chance Regina could be alive," Tidwell said to Deetz. "You were right about Meander Falls, that's where we start. Jeanette's giving us the keys to the camper van. She thinks it will be there. I told her we'll be confiscating the Jeep."

Deetz glanced back and Brodie was staring at Jeanette with a menacing glare. But, with her arms crossed, she wandered a few feet here and there, rocked her shoulders back and forth, looking at the trees, the street—everything but her husband.

Tidwell said, "Ambulance is due any minute. We need to have a medic look at Brodie, just to be on the safe side. Let's have Googan take him back to the precinct and get him booked in. I'm going to send the two officers with you to the campsite. I have to get back."

"Got it," Deetz said, turning to return to Googan and Brodie.

"Wayne," Tidwell called.

Deetz stopped and looked back.

"Jeanette's ready to tell everything." Tidwell made an O with his mouth shook his head. "There've been many women. She's got meticulous descriptions. She's been a victim, to say the least. We've got him, Wayne. He'll never see the light of day. Quite a way to finish out. Good work."

36

—————

AT SOME TIME after 8 p.m. on Christmas Eve, the Deetz home was bustling with talk, laughter, and activity—and carols playing softly in the background. The whole family, along with Randall and Roxanne, had enjoyed Chinese take-out, and then they'd gone in several cars to the candlelight service at the Deetz's church, which had delighted Wayne and Joanie. Now, everyone was scattered around a blazing fire in the den, some sitting on the floor and others on couches and in comfy chairs.

Deetz and Joanie sat close on the couch holding hands, he with his socked feet resting on the coffee table. He was content to sit back and take it all in, so grateful for times like these when the whole family was together, and everyone was healthy. He tried never to take even one day for granted and silently thanked Jesus for the day's provisions.

He thought of Brodie Enoch in the lock-up on Christmas Eve. He'd been denied bail that morning during his initial appearance before the magistrate. He was formally charged with breaking and entering the Deetz home, robbery, and eavesdropping using a recording device. In addition, thanks to Jeanette's statements, he was being charged for domestic battery, psychological and emotional abuse, coercive control, and physical abuse. Brodie had pleaded not guilty to all charges.

When Deetz and the two officers had arrived at Meander Falls after Brodie's arrest, they'd found the camper van, zip ties, a bottle of Chloroform, obvious signs of a struggle, and even blood stains—but no sign of Regina Hart. The forensics team found a myriad of hair and blood samples and DNA evidence in the camper van, the Jeep, and in the Enoch residence. Although Regina had not been found, her DNA, hair, and fingerprints were located in all three places, and Brodie was being held on kidnapping charges, to which he had also pled not guilty.

Just as Howard Googan had surmised, Jeanette Enoch confessed that there had been other women whom—just like Regina Hart—had been kidnapped, physically and emotionally terrorized, and discarded without a trace. DNA, blood, and hair found in Brodie's vehicles was still being examined by Portland Police, and Deetz and Googan hoped matches would be found from the women who had disappeared in Carson City, Bakersfield, Sacramento, and who knew where else. With Deetz turning in his badge in a few days, he reflected on what an achievement it would be to go out having put away a sick serial killer.

Deetz dialed back into the conversation in the room.

Tammy had just asked Kristen how far along she was in her pregnancy.

"Let's see, right now I'm just about at the end of my first trimester, thirteen weeks," Kristen said, with a hand on her tummy.

"So, when is the due date again?" J.P. asked.

"June seventeenth," Kristen said.

"It'll be here before you know it," Joanie said.

"How are you feeling?" Tammy asked. "Sick at all?"

Deetz was thinking Tammy and J.P. could be married and planning their own family by this time next year.

"I've been really tired, to be honest," Kristen said. "Other than that, feeling pretty good. Not a lot of food sounds good to me."

"Especially the smell of meat," Brandon said with a chuckle.

"Oh, I can't stand the smell of meat," Kristen said. "Ugh, it makes me sick."

"Raw or cooked?" Tammy asked.

"Any of it!" Kristen said.

"That's why she had the veggie fried rice," Brandon said.

"I felt the same way, Kristen," said Joanie. "I remember when I was pregnant with one of the kids, I cried while I was browning meat, it just smelled so bad to me."

They all laughed.

"The one thing I crave like crazy right now is Chick-fil-A biscuits," Kristen said, pointing at Leena. "That's about the only thing."

Leena's eyes lit up and her mouth opened wide. "CFA biscuits? Are you for real? I love those things, too. I wish I could bring you some from work but, unfortunately, we only get a discount on break meals, shakes, and specialty drinks."

"That's okay, Brandon doesn't mind treating me to a biscuit now and then, do you sweetie?"

"That's what I'm here for," Brandon said.

When the conversation began to delve more deeply into favorite foods and restaurants, Randall, who was seated in a chair next to Deetz, tapped him and said quietly, "I read that story about the Good Samaritan."

"Really?" Deetz was pleasantly surprised and observed that the conversation in the room was loud enough so that the two men could have a discussion without being eavesdropped upon. "What'd you think?"

Randall chuckled. "It was deep, for sure. Bottom line, the people who should have helped him didn't—like the priest."

Deetz nodded and thought about it. "Yeah, and the whole thing really came back down to where Jesus said, 'Love your neighbor as yourself.' We're supposed to love and do for others exactly what we would want done for us. Treat others how you want to be treated, no matter who they are."

"But the guy testing Jesus, it said he wanted to validate himself when he asked, 'Who is my neighbor?'"

"Right," Deetz said. "He was hoping Jesus would say something like, 'Well, your neighbor is the person who lives directly next door to you, who you like very much."

They both laughed.

"At the end of it, Jesus asked the guy, 'Well, which one of the three was a true neighbor to the guy who got robbed?'" Randall said.

Deetz nodded and let Randall finish.

"And the guy said, 'It was the one who had mercy on him.'"

"Go and do likewise," Deetz said.

Both men sat there in silence for a moment, nodding, trying to grasp what that meant, and how it should impact how they lived.

"I want to be like that," Randall said. "I really want to change."

"I want to be like that, too," Deetz said. "But we're not like that, naturally."

"Yeah, but you've been like that—with me. You've been extremely kind to us when we deserved the opposite."

"That's because I would have wanted the same done for me if I were in your shoes."

Their conversation dropped off momentarily while the others continued to rattle on in festive chatter.

"Plus," Deetz chimed back in, "I couldn't have done that if Christ wasn't living in me. The sinful me has no mercy. But, because he lives in me, I have *his* mercy."

"See, I don't get that." Randall leaned forward and rested his big wrists on his knees. "How can Christ live in you? I just . . . I don't understand it."

Deetz got chills. He couldn't believe Randall was asking such things. He prayed God would give him the right words. He leaned over closer to Randall and said quietly, "You invite him into your life, into your heart. You believe in him—the fact that he so bravely and mercifully went to the cross to die to forgive our sins."

"I want to believe," Randall said. "But I don't know anything about this stuff. I never went to church. Plus, the things I've done. You don't know the half of it."

"That doesn't matter. God knows, and he's still pulling at your heartstrings, Randall. It's obvious. He's drawing you. He's knocking at your door. All you have to do is open it and say, 'Yes, come into my life.'"

"I do want that."

"He wants that. He wants *you*, Randall. He wants to live in you, to protect you, to guide you. And when you believe, his Holy Spirit comes to live in you, to be your helper. That's what the Bible says. And when that happens, your life starts to bear the fruit of his Spirit—things you can't produce on your own, like love and joy, peace and patience, kindness, goodness . . ."

Randall's eyes glistened. He stared at Deetz. His bottom lip quivered ever so slightly. He nodded resolutely and whispered, "I do believe."

Deetz's eyes filled with emotion as he felt a huge grin break out on his face. "Just think," he whispered, "you became a Christian on Christmas Eve."

Randall laughed quietly and wiped his eyes on the sleeve of his shirt.

"My, my," Roxanne piped up, "you two are having quite the intimate conversation over there. Are you going to include us?"

Deetz's phone vibrated in his back pocket.

Who calls on Christmas Eve?

"I'll tell you about it later," Randall said to Roxanne.

Deetz leaned forward, got his phone out, and examined the screen.

It was Sergeant Tidwell calling.

"Hey, Sarge, Merry Christmas," Deetz answered.

"Hey Wayne, sorry to bother you. You sitting down?"

"I am, actually."

"Regina Hart's been found—alive."

"Where?" Deetz shot to his feet and walked out of the den so he could hear more clearly. "When?"

"A family camping at Meander Falls heard whimpering coming from the woods. They thought it was an injured animal. She was buried in a shallow grave. She'd been strangled. He must've thought she was dead."

"Is she talking? Could she say who did it?" Deetz said, looking out the front window at the night rain, imagining that poor woman buried alive out in the elements.

"It was traumatic, as you can imagine. She's still in shock and recovering from the cold and hunger. But the doctor I talked to said he's optimistic she's going to make a full recovery."

"Thank God."

"Indeed," Tidwell said. "See, Wayne, it's times like this, if you were my police chaplain, you could go be with her while she recovers. You'd be ministering to her and getting us answers at the same time."

"Yeah, all on Christmas Eve. Joanie would love that."

Tidwell laughed.

"You're not gonna give up on that chaplain thing, are you?" Deetz said.

There was a long pause.

"I'm just going to miss you, that's all," Tidwell said. "You're one of the good ones, Wayne."

WHAT'S NEXT FROM CRESTON?

Creston is currently working on brand new thriller. He is still contemplating whether or not to write another book in the Signs of Life Series. If you have an opinion on that, shoot him an email via his website: **www.CrestonMapes.com**.

For your reading pleasure, to follow is a description and excerpt from Creston's all-time bestselling book, *Fear Has a Name,* book one in The Crittendon Files series.

A Name from the Past. A Love That Never Died.
A Nightmare That Just Began.

Granger Meade has returned to Trenton City, Ohio.

Scarred by a childhood with religious zealot parents and bullied into isolation, Granger has never forgotten the one person who showed him kindness—Pamela Wagner. She made him feel seen. Human. Loved.

Now, twenty years later, Pamela is happily married to investigative reporter Jack Crittendon. Jack is consumed by a high-profile case involving a missing pastor, a mysterious suicide note, and a storm of church scandal.

But when Granger crosses paths with Pamela again, something inside him snaps. The past collides violently with the present—and Pamela's life hangs in the balance.

Jack is thrown into a desperate race against time to save his wife from a man driven by obsession, memory, and madness.

Perfect for fans of psychological thrillers, faith-based suspense, and stories with deep emotional stakes.

Chapter One

The husky man lurking outside the front door of Pamela Crittendon's house carried a black leather satchel, like a doctor's bag.

Hiding behind a column between the foyer and dining room, Pamela could see the stranger through one of the narrow vertical windows situated on each side of the door.

His face was hardened and pasty, with tiny eyes and a thatch of curly red hair. He wore all black, from his T-shirt and leather vest to his jeans and cowboy boots. And he stood uncomfortably close to the door.

The doorbell rang a third time.

Pamela's head buzzed.

Backlit by the midafternoon sunlight, the man turned toward the street. Covering half his face with a blocky, gloved hand, he shifted his huge frame from one foot to the other. Then he turned and rapped hard at the glass, knocking the wind out of Pamela.

"Who's at the door, Mommy?" Seven-year-old Rebecca appeared at the top of the stairs wearing pink plastic high heels, a red sequined dress, and a purple boa. Bumping into her from behind was her five-year-old sister, Faye, who wore a long white dress, a furry brown stole, and turquoise gloves that went up to her armpits.

"I'm not sure," Pamela said, her voice constricted. "Go back to the media room and play. Hurry, go on."

Taking a deep breath, she fought her way through a force field of fear to within three feet of the door and made herself yell deeply, sharply, "Who is it?" She searched the man through the glass.

He clamped the doorknob. "Open!"

The hardware made a sickening racket.

"Get out of here!" Her stomach turned. "I'm calling the police!"

She rushed for the phone in the kitchen.

Boom!

Pamela halted, turned toward the noise at the door, and gawked in horror as the stranger bent over and drove his shoulder—the size of a medicine ball—into the door, splintering the wood frame.

BOOM!

"Mo-omm-my?" Rebecca cried from the top of the steps. She was clutching Peep, her favorite doll. "Who's banging at the door?"

"Get down here, *now*. Both of you!" But as soon as the words left her mouth, Pamela realized she couldn't wait. She shot up the stairs, swept up both girls, and plunged back down.

Each frantic step felt like an adrenaline-laced nightmare.

As they passed within four feet of the front door, the glass shattered.

"Ahhh!" Pamela shrieked, dashing away from the eerie closeness of the intruder, hoping the girls wouldn't see the man, but their little eyes were huge. Rebecca let loose a terror-ridden scream. Faye was frozen. Pamela kept going, like a soldier bolting through a minefield, with both girls locked in her arms, one thought in her brain: *Get out.*

She heard him reaching in, groping for the bolt lock.

This cannot be happening.

Dropping the girls to their feet, she flipped the lock to the back door and slammed it open.

She heard glass crunching beneath the man's boots.

"Wait!" he called.

Pamela grabbed the girls' little hands and rocketed through the door onto the screened porch.

She could feel him coming, maybe fifteen feet behind.

She kicked the screened door open.

They hit fresh air.

And grass.

Run.

Faster than you ever have.

Pamela flew toward the neighbors' house, ripping at the girls' hands, feeling as if their little legs had left the ground, as if they were the dollies now.

Across the flat green lawn they dashed, the girls whimpering and squealing with each panicked stride.

Without knocking, Pamela tried the handle, found it open, and burst into the Sweeneys' house with the girls—slamming the door and dead-bolting it behind her.

Tommy Sweeney shot out of his office and stopped when he saw them. "Pamela? What on earth is going on?"

"A man broke in . . . while we were there . . ." It was difficult to breathe. Her heart hurt. Her brain banged against her skull. Her neck and shoulders felt torn from the weight of the girls. "He may be coming . . . check, Tommy. He was right behind us." She stroked the girls' hair with trembling hands and drew them tight against her body.

Tommy shot in motion toward the kitchen window, reaching for the phone on his belt clip. "I see him out back. He's turning around . . . He's going back in."

Pamela could only nod, relieved that at least someone else had seen him.

"It's okay. You're safe now." Tommy punched at the screen of his cell phone and looked out the window. "Tell me what happened."

"He rang the doorbell a bunch, then pounded. I told him to go away, that I was calling the police—"

"Did you?"

She shook her head. "No time. He broke the glass at the front door and came in."

When he'd shattered the glass, found the bolt lock and entered, there must have been only ten feet between them. Ten feet and how many seconds? Three? Maybe four? If she'd delayed only that long in getting the girls, the monster would have had them. And done what? To her? *To them?*

"Jesus took care of us," she whispered and nestled the girls close.

Tommy was still peering out the window, focused on her backyard.

"Do you see him?" Pamela asked.

"No. He's still inside." He held up an index finger and spoke into the phone. "Yes, ma'am, we've had a break-in next door to the address I'm calling from . . . I will in a minute, but you should know the intruder is still on the property . . . *hurry.*"

Get FEAR HAS A NAME
and all of Creston's novels on Amazon.

ABOUT THE AUTHOR

Creston Mapes grew up in northeast Ohio, where he has fond memories of living with his family of five in the upstairs portion of his dad's early American furniture store - The Weathervane Shop. Creston was not a good student, but the one natural talent he possessed was writing.

He set type by hand and cranked out his own neighborhood newspaper as a kid, then went on to graduate with a degree in journalism from Bowling Green State University. Creston was a newspaper reporter and photographer in Ohio and Florida, then moved to Atlanta, Georgia, for a job as a creative copywriter.

Creston served for a stint as a creative director, but quickly learned he was not cut out for management. He went out on his own as a freelance writer in 1991 and, over the next 30 years, did work for Chick-fil-A, Coca-Cola, The Weather Channel, Oracle, ABC-TV, TNT Sports, colleges and universities, ad agencies, and more. He's ghost-written more than ten non-fiction books.

Creston has penned many contemporary thrillers, achieved Amazon Bestseller status multiple times, and had one of his novels (*Nobody*) optioned as a major motion picture.

Creston married his fourth-grade sweetheart, Patty, and they have four amazing adult children. Creston loves his part-time job as an usher at local venues where he gets to see all the latest-greatest concerts and sporting events. He enjoys reading, fishing, thrifting, bocci, painting, bowling, pickleball, time with his family, and dates with his wife.

All of Creston's books are available on Amazon in ebook, paperback, hardback and audio.

To keep informed of special deals, giveaways, new releases, and exclusive updates from Creston, sign up for his newsletter via his website: **www.CrestonMapes.com.**

SIGNS OF LIFE SERIES
Signs of Life
Let My Daughter Go
I Pick You
Charm Artist
Son & Shield
Secrets in Shadows
Who Is My Neighbor?

THE CRITTENDON FILES
Fear Has a Name
Poison Town
Sky Zone

ROCK STAR CHRONICLES
Dark Star: Confessions of a Rock Idol
Full Tilt

STAND ALONE THRILLERS
Celebrity Pastor
I Am In Here
Nobody